MW00799937

GRINGO JOE

A novel by

J D Davis

ELM HILL

A Division of
HarperCollins Christian Publishing

www.elmhillbooks.com

Gringo Joe

Published in Nashville, Tennessee, by Elm Hill, an imprint of Thomas Nelson. Elm Hill and Thomas Nelson are registered trademarks of HarperCollins Christian Publishing, Inc.

Elm Hill titles may be purchased in bulk for educational, business, fund-raising, or sales promotional use. For information, please e-mail SpecialMarkets@ThomasNelson.com.

Library of Congress Cataloging-in-Publication Data

Library Congress Control Number: 2018933346

ISBN 978-1-595543523 (Paperback)
ISBN 978-1-595543554 (Hardbound)
ISBN 978-1-595544933 (eBook)

For my wife, Keri, sent by God as a reminder of His grace.
Thank you for praying and believing.

Acknowledgment

Steve Walker, pastor, teacher, author, confidant, encourager, and *mi buen hermano*: thank you, Steve, for all those cups of dark, fresh-roasted coffee, and warm cinnamon rolls. Taking shelter from the Oregon rains and listening to your wisdom has encouraged me to be a better man.

Gino Elsea, a soldier and warrior who did "God's work" for forty years: thank you, my friend, for your insight and advice, and for doing what few could and what the rest of us would not.

To the men and women who wear the uniforms and believe freedom from tyranny, evil and fear, for all mankind, is worth the risk of their lives. I am thankful, and we owe you our gratitude.

According to the United Nations, human trafficking is one of the fastest growing criminal enterprises in the world. Human trafficking affects over 5.5 million children, most of whom are sold as sex slaves. It is a multibillion-dollar industry and only getting larger. According to the advocacy group Free the Slaves, there are more slaves on Earth today than there have been at any other point in history. Think about that: Over 21 million lives are affected by the horrors of slavery every single day.

Thank you to the courageous men and women—many risking their lives—who give generously and fight tirelessly to rescue men, women, boys and girls from an unfathomable hell. God bless you.

Table of Contents

The deepest I have loved, the most I have surrendered,
and certainly the hardest I have fallen was in the arms of a
woman.
Yet it is the battle, in fellowship of noble men, where iron
sharpens iron, doubt surrenders, and souls find courage.

J D Davis

CHAPTER 1

A Mexican, a Tractor, and a One-Legged Chicken

It is one of life's great joys to see someone laughing so hard, when they can barely stand as they gasp for a breath, wiping away the tears streaming down their face. It's often contagious, infecting innocent bystanders.

Duffy owned a bar on Orange Avenue, a popular watering hole for locals. He had sufficient cause to justify his usual melancholy demeanor, but today he was trying to get his breath and wipe his eyes from the hardest laugh he'd enjoyed in a decade. A young man sitting astride one of his stools had told a story so incredibly funny, once he finally stopped laughing, the barkeep yelled for quiet. Before the young man could object, Duffy hollered, "Gather 'round one and all and listen up. If it's not the best story you've ever heard, your next beer is on the house."

At the mention of free beer, twenty patrons looked up from their tables and stools.

The young man wore jeans and his tee shirt showed off a powerful physique, not the gym-kind but from a lifetime of hard work. Although his hair was long and well past a trim, and his face days past a shave, the lad had an easy smile and eyes as warm and inviting as a roaring fireplace on a cold winter's eve.

He had no desire to repeat the story, for it had been spontaneous and personal, shared with a man he respected. Unlike many of the patrons, he hadn't come to deafen the shrill of demons but to hear the whisper of wisdom. He had questions common men couldn't answer, but he figured Duffy and few men like him could. Because the bartender was a good soul and listened intently to all the young man's concerns, he reluctantly agreed to one more telling of his tale.

Duffy, childishly giddy to hear it again, insisted the lad turn and sit on the bar, facing the semi-interested crowd. Some rolled their eyes, expecting a drunk to tell an off-colored joke, but once he began a hush fell over the room, as everyone began to lean in and hang on every word. There was nothing loud or boisterous about the stranger, but instead he spoke with a quiet, resolute voice. The story, he assured them, was true and involved a Mexican named Jose, a tractor without brakes, and a one-legged chicken.

His name was Joe and, unbeknownst to the crowd, he was one day away from changing his life forever. His eyes danced, his arms swirled above his head, and, within minutes, every last soul was captivated by the rhythm and enchantment of his voice. Well before it ended, folks were wide-eyed and spellbound. Reaching its crescendo, all who were able were on their feet, laughing hilariously and applauding. There were offers of free beer, jobs, and at least one proposal of marriage. Fresh drinks were ordered, backs were slapped, and yet, before anyone realized, Joe had slipped away. He turned up his collar against the advancing Pacific fog and walked for miles, contemplating all he had learned. The lad was gone but his story lingered, retold again and again, until Duffy turned out the lights and locked the door.

CHAPTER 2

Coffee and Wine (Four-and-a-Half Years Later)

Michele Randle was the daughter of a hardworking Swedish dairyman and grew up with a sense of humor that was, well, somewhere between awkward and hard to explain. She did, however, inherit her father's work ethic, instinctive logic, and her mother's extremely good looks. After a bachelor's degree in history and prepping for law school, Michele, or Mel as everyone called her, did a tour of combat—at least that is how she referred to her three months as an intern for a San Francisco congresswoman. The chief of staff recognized her exceptional talent and begged her to stay, but the environment of Washington DC had shocked and disgusted Mel. Regardless of being raised in a Christian home with conservative values, like many college students, Mel's pendulum swung from right to left at Stanford University. However, working in DC, for whom she later called "A leftist, self-serving, maniacal lunatic," the pendulum had settled a bit more to the center.

After her graduation from Stanford Law, Mel passed the California Bar with exceptional ease and then, to quote her brother, "Mel was possessed by an alien being, which short-circuited her common sense and robbed her of a promising financial future."

Mel was disciplined, sensible, and implemented her steely-eyed focus on well-thought-out goals and objectives. However, in celebration of her graduation and to consider the multiple offers of employment, she did the first spontaneous and impetuous thing she'd done in over seven years—she drove to a small town in Oregon and rented a cozy studio apartment. It was furnished, walking distance to restaurants, and overlooked a small vineyard on a nearby hillside. The town was a random choice, discovered as she searched for gas and food. The exit sign mentioned wine tours and a fly-fishing wilderness. The thundering river still bellowing from the Cascade snowmelt and beautiful rolling hills that blended with fir trees and vineyards reminded her of a shire where Hobbits dwelled and mythical legends were born.

She was finishing a sandwich when she saw a woman putting out a FOR RENT sign, so she inquired. The lady was friendly, the place was clean and cheap, so she leased it for a month. Mel knew she would never stay that long, but the price was right and the town had a slow, mellow vibe; exactly what she was looking for. She read mindless novels, played Candy Crush, ate pizza, and discovered her true love—fresh shots of espresso buried beneath a splash of vanilla and layers of steamed whole milk. It makes sense: in a state where it's either raining or considering it, coffee flows from pots, spigots, and espresso machines on every corner, but what ends up in a cup varies from something black and hot to a life-changing, mind-altering experience.

It was late afternoon when she strolled into the beautiful artisan cottage, home to an espresso shop and bakery. The smell of freshly roasted coffee beans mixed with warm cinnamon rolls and marionberry scones was intoxicating. With no more deadlines, classes, or papers due, Mel threw caution to the wind and decided to try one of everything. Two hours later, after the coming and going of dozens of patrons, the handsome barista with the greenest eyes she'd ever seen approached her table. He tilted his head and looked at her for a moment with a bit of a curt smile.

"Ma'am, I'm afraid it's my responsibility to cut you off. There will be no more sugar or caffeine."

"Oh, my God!" exclaimed Mel. "I've been jabbering nonstop for over an hour... to complete strangers. You're right, I definitely need something to eat besides a third scone; those things should be illegal. Forgive me if I've embarrassed myself."

After finishing the last of her third latte, she stood to leave. Helping with her chair, Joe looked down with those dreamy eyes and, in his hushed yet confident manner, said, "I think you've earned a good salad and glass of our local Tempranillo."

"Is that an invitation?" Still buzzing from at least six shots of espresso, she didn't wait for an answer. "Actually I would love to, but I don't think we've been introduced."

"You're right; my apologies—I'm Joe."

"Hello, I'm Michele but I answer better to Mel. Wait! Do you mean Joe as in Gringo Joe, like the sign out front? Are you that Joe?"

"Guilty as charged. If it's alright, I'll swing by around five?"

"Well, okay, I guess, sure... my address is...."

Joe held up his hand and smiled.

"It's a small town; I know where you're staying. It'll be semicasual but bring a wrap, we'll dine outside."

For the last several years Mel had kept her head down and studied relentlessly with very few distractions, especially from men. Oh, she was a brown-eyed beauty with thick chestnut hair, and there had been many invitations, most of which had been kindly refused.

Walking back to her studio, Mel suddenly realized she had a date; at least it felt like a date. No doubt Joe was a fine specimen of a man, with eyes big, green, and deep enough to drown in.

Oh well, she thought, *I'm just passing through and, after all, he's just a cute, uncomplicated barista. What's the harm?*

She slipped on a pair of Escada jeans and a colorful peasant top that showed off her figure. Staring into a mirror she said, "Goodness, Mel, you look marvelous," just as a car door slammed.

Mel was more than surprised when the "barista" showed up wearing a crisp white shirt under what was obviously an expensive sport coat. But when she walked out and saw a vintage 1962 Corvette convertible, her jaw dropped.

"Wow! Coffee drinkers must be better tippers than I imagined."

Joe shrugged his shoulder and helped Mel with her jacket. He closed her door and the two sped down the highway with "I Need a Miracle" by Third Day blaring from the speakers.

When Joe suggested a local Tempranillo, Mel never imagined they would enjoy it on a beautiful stone porch overlooking a magnificent vineyard. And when the owners of the magnificent vineyard came out with a Tuscany salad, fresh bread, and two bottles of wine, Joe stood.

"Mel, I'd like you to meet my parents, Cade and Elizabeth Chandler."

"Call me Lizzie—everybody does, and we all call my husband Drummer."

Drummer and Lizzie were gracious, humble, and, with roots from the South, as hospitable as a Charleston quilting circle.

Joe hardly said a word but sipped and ate with a discerning eye as his parents began opening the very interesting box named Mel Randle.

"Mr. Chandler—"

"It's Drummer," he exclaimed to her. "Please call me Drummer."

"All right, Drummer it is. I was wondering how you came by such an interesting name?"

Drummer and Joe locked eyes; Joe smiled and shook his head.

"It is your life, Dad. You own it, you survived it, and it's your story to tell."

Drummer cleared his throat for what appeared to be the beginning of a long narrative, when Lizzie interceded.

"Honey, for over a decade my heartthrob sitting over there was the drummer for a very famous Southern rock band. Perhaps you've heard of the Ozark Midnight Dance Band?"

Mel blushed, apologized, and took another long sip of her very good wine.

"No matter," injected Drummer. "We were legends long before anyone ever heard of Stevie Ray Vaughan or Joan Jett."

Mel shifted uncomfortably in her seat because, again, the names were vaguely familiar but she couldn't immediately recall any of their songs.

Growing up on a dairy the work was hard and early, and if there was any music at all, it was one of two kinds—country or Western.

"Surely you've heard of the Pretenders or Tom Petty and the Heartbreakers," Drummer said, slightly deflated.

"Yes!" exclaimed Mel, "I have heard of him. I loved 'Free Fallin'.'"

Drummer suddenly perked up. "Yeah, you bet I watched him sing it in El Paso from backstage. Yes sir, we even played with ZZ Top on their first of several farewell tours. I know you've listened to some floor-stomping ZZ Top?"

Seeing her discomfort, Joe said quietly, "Would you care to take a walk?"

Seizing the opportunity to stop offending Drummer, Mel accepted and the two excused themselves and strolled away into a beautiful setting sun.

"My, my, my, did you see the way Joe looked at that girl?" Lizzie whispered with a pleasant sigh.

"Yes . . . I . . . did, and I think there is more to the lovely Ms. Mel than meets the eye."

"Oh, I like her too," said Lizzie.

"Well, let's see. It makes sense your mom is called Lizzie, and now, with some context, I understand why your father is called Drummer, but how in the world did you end up as Gringo Joe?"

"It's a really long story and I don't want to. . . ."

"I absolutely love stories, Joe, please, and no shortcuts, I want all the details."

Joe gazed toward the darkening sky and let his mind slip comfortably into his childhood.

"One of my earliest memories is me sitting at Dad's drums, banging away as Mom applauded wildly. I also remember the long absences when Dad was on tour. The reality for a rock star," he said shyly, "is a wife and child back home doing everything without you."

Drummer Chandler had been a gifted percussionist—maybe even a prodigy—but as it turned out, perhaps his greatest talents were his ability to invest well and his immense love for Lizzie and Joe.

Before walking away from stardom on his thirty-third birthday, he purchased two hundred acres of farmland in the rolling hills of Western Oregon, and then he bought a gazillion shares of Apple stock for ninety-seven cents a share. Folks thought he was crazy.

"Mom and Dad were both raised in the South," Joe continued. "Mom was from Sugarland, Texas, and Dad was an Arkansas farm boy who went to Baylor University on a music scholarship. It was actually my dad's cousin, Twissle, who started the band with a couple of friends and, as it turned out, they had talent."

"Twissle—really?" asked Mel.

"Yeah; apparently, he couldn't pronounce his 'Ws' as a little boy, and 'whistle' came out 'twissle' and the name stuck. That's the South for you. Be careful of an embarrassing idiosyncrasy or you might wear it for the rest of your life."

The band's original percussionist came down with mono just before a summer road trip. Cade Chandler reluctantly agreed to fill in until school started, and he just never left. Twissle wrote the words, Drummer did the scoring and composition, and before they knew it, they were on tour with several hit records. Fame came fast, but the real money was from touring, year after year, with some of the biggest names in rock music. Few bands, with all their egos and girlfriends, survived more than one tour, but beating all the odds the Ozark Midnight Dance Band rode the wave for almost fourteen years. However, one day it did end, and everyone knew it was time. When they parted, they parted as friends, and by all accounts, another miracle.

One evening in early May, much to the delight of Lizzie, Drummer showed up, unpacked his bags, and said he was going to be a farmer. At the time they were living close to Lizzie's mom and dad in Texas, but within weeks Drummer bought a diesel truck and a big fifth wheel RV and towed it to Oregon. During all the lonely hours and downtime as a road warrior, Drummer had meticulously planned his second life, starting with a vineyard.

A year earlier when the band was playing at a music festival in Santa Cruz, California, Drummer rented a car and drove to Napa where he met Jose Palmero. Jose was a wine-making genius. While his English was only tolerable, he was a vintner, a chemist, a farmer, welder, mechanic, and even a practicing alchemist. Drummer and Jose had a long discussion involving several bottles of wine, a dream, a vision, and money. The money sealed the deal, and Jose agreed to move his wife to Oregon just as soon as Drummer found them a house.

To everyone's surprise, Sonata added, "We come when the check you give ... it is good ... no problemo."

"We still owned a home in Texas, but our hearts and future were here. I ran barefoot through these fields while Mom, Dad, Jose, and Sonata planted grapes. Jose, or Joe as everyone started calling him, was a Renaissance man—smart, animated, and kind to me, so I became his shadow. I held vines while he tied them, handed him wrenches when he worked on our tractor, and even learned to sing in Spanish. In the evenings, Jose would play his guitar and Sonata would sing as we all huddled around a campfire. Soon after we built the first barn we started on our house, added some laborers, and the dream began to take shape. It was a delightful time, but whenever anyone yelled for Joe, we both came running. I was probably ten years old when we walked into a local hardware store full of people. As we entered, the merchant said, '*Here they come, Joe and little Gringo Joe,*' and the rest is history."

Mel walked and drank in the spellbinding story as easily as she had the delightful wine. There was something honest and enchanting about his voice. Never in her wildest imagination had she expected the barista to be so charming, but charming did not begin to explain the layers of Joe Chandler.

"Enough about me," Joe said, embarrassed that he had droned on. "What about you? What's next for California's newest law grad?"

Mel had barely mentioned it at dinner, as she had barely mentioned much at all about herself. She exhaled slowly and averted the question with another question of her own—a trait, which Joe noticed, she practiced with ease.

"So, coffee and wine, how exactly did that happen?"

Joe was capable of dodging questions himself. "Well, a story for another time I suppose. Speaking of which, is there any chance you'd accompany me to a fundraiser this Saturday evening? It's hosted by our mayor and his wife, Jillian. It's a nice dinner and you'd save me the embarrassment of explaining myself to the ladies in attendance who all know a nice girl I should meet."

Mel didn't know why she hesitated, but it was long enough to be awkward. Joe quickly let her off the hook.

"Hey, no worries if you have other plans; just stop by for a coffee and let me know. Speaking of which, I open early tomorrow, so if you don't mind, I should probably call it a night."

He and Mel made the slow walk back to his car with hardly a word.

"I liked the music," she said. "Could we hear some more on the way back?"

"Of course," he said, wondering if somewhere in the otherwise pleasant evening he had offended her. Not a word had been spoken in the car—just the raspy voice of Mac Powell—but when Joe stopped, Mel put her hand on his and said she'd get the door, then leaned over and kissed his cheek.

"Perfect. It was a perfect evening. Thank you, and tell your parents I'm sorry I didn't say goodbye." Then she disappeared inside.

CHAPTER 3

In Search of the Extraordinary

When Joe transferred from Cal Poly in San Luis Obispo to Biola University in La Mirada, California, he and Drummer argued so furiously Lizzie thought it would come to blows. The vineyard, now featured in magazines and shipping its award-winning Tempranillo and Pinot Noir all over the world, needed constant attention. Drummer had always assumed Joe would fill the void. After all, besides himself and perhaps Jose Palmero, his son knew more about the operation of Segundo Vida Vineyards than anyone did. *Segundo vida* in Spanish simply means *second life*, and for Joe that was really the rub. Since he was eight years old the vineyard had been his only life, and now he planned to see what options the rest of the world offered. The vineyard was hard work, and Joe had taken to it like a hungry dog to a bone. He had an inquisitive mind and was always asking questions—or worse, questioning his father's decisions. He understood the science perfectly but it was the farming, the planting, and harvesting which Joe loved. Picking the grapes with his family and neighbors was a spiritual experience. At the end of most days, Joe would slip away to a quiet place, make sure no one was watching, and give thanks to the God of the harvest. In Joe's mind, the connection between a vineyard and the spiritual was as natural as a storm and a rainbow.

Joe's infatuation with the God of the Bible had begun in Texas. His grandmother, known as Mémé, was a fiery French Cajun and a devout Catholic. However, his grandpa—a soft-spoken, six-foot, five-inch Texan whom everyone called Hoss—was a Protestant and a masterful expositor of the Bible. His given name was Harmon Littlefield, and while he owned a successful tractor dealership in South Texas, he much preferred to tell folks about the love of Jesus. On any given Sunday, you could find Hoss in a Baptist, Methodist, Presbyterian, or Holiness church teaching the Bible. Hoss never put too much stock in the name over the door, so in an area where poor churches couldn't afford a full-time preacher, you'd find Hoss. He had married, buried, counseled, and, from time to time, fed hundreds of poor Texans. Mémé would faithfully attend Saturday evening mass, then follow Hoss from church to church, often yelling *"Amen!"* from a front-row pew. Much to Hoss and Mémé's disappointment, their daughter, Elizabeth, had rebelled and married a musician; but all was forgiven when Joe was born. They had practically raised their grandson while Drummer was on the road and had instilled into him a reverent respect of things holy. Lizzie knew the Bible backwards and forwards but she marveled at her son who, from an early age, had the quiet, personal relationship with God that she'd traded for a handsome rock star.

When Joe graduated from high school, Drummer hadn't asked his son about his plans or his dreams, but instead made implications and assumptions. Joe loved his parents and didn't want to disappoint them or the Palmeros, whom he loved like family. Regardless, there were things calling and itches, life at the vineyard were not scratching.

Joe had been an agricultural engineering major at Cal Poly, but after transferring to Biola, a wise counselor suggested political science or international studies—he fell in love with both. During his junior year, he was selected to do a semester of Middle Eastern studies in Amman, Jordan.

Joe always went home for Christmas and spent a couple of summers helping with the vineyard, but he was still hearing distant voices, and his Dad could see it.

Joe crammed a great deal into four-and-a-half years and when he graduated, he did so with honors. Lizzie watched him walk and take his diploma, but his father had an important meeting and wasn't able to make it. After a celebratory dinner with his mom and friends, Joe drove Lizzie back to the Orange County Airport. He said he needed to "kick over a few rocks" and asked her not to worry. He also assured her that he and his father loved each other, and time would be a great healer. After a few tears, she told him she was attending church again and would pray for him every day, then kissed him goodbye.

To his credit, Joe had done his homework. After long hours of research, he prayed and began his quest. Though he was looking for direction, his mission was not about companies, jobs, or career paths. Joe's research was about men, not average men, not men who led unextraordinary lives but great men.

He drove to Utah to meet Ben, a man who lived in a used 36-foot RV that sat under the overhang of a large barn somewhere close to nowhere. Ben was an inventor and owned over 300 registered patents. His last one was an inexpensive water pump that brought clean underground water to over 450,000 drought-stricken people in Africa. When his wife, Celeste, died of a tropical disease she contracted while helping others, Ben gave away tens of millions of dollars to dig more wells and buy mosquito nets for at-risk children on three continents. Joe liked Ben, and Ben hugged him when he left and told him he'd find his way.

In Birmingham, Alabama, Joe sat under a large pecan tree with Leroy Swain. Joe read about Mr. Swain three years earlier and wanted to meet him, so he did. LeRoy had been tied behind a pickup truck and dragged down a gravel road as two men in the back threw empty beer bottles at him. The incident had left him crippled for the rest of his life but not broken. The men were eventually arrested, and while the driver shot himself instead of going to prison, the two brothers served thirteen years of a twenty-year sentence. Donnie Ray and Elmer Clabber would have served their full terms if not for Leroy Swain. After two years of skin graft operations and learning to walk again, Leroy started visiting the two brothers in prison. First he told them he forgave them just to get their attention; then he told them about a remarkable carpenter from Galilee... every other Sunday afternoon... for eleven years. He repeatedly went to the parole board on their behalf until they were finally released into his custody. They had no family, no money, and no chance... but for Leroy. He and his wife took them in, fed and loved them, and treated them as family. Today, the three men run a half-house, a men's Bible study, a chapter of AAA, and they take turns preaching at a small Baptist Church on the outskirts of Birmingham. It is an all-Black church.

The last man Joe visited owned a bar on the west side of Coronado, California. Duffy had taken a liking to him, especially after hearing the funniest story he'd ever heard about a one-legged chicken and a Mexican. Duffy, an ex-Navy SEAL, had more scars inside than out. He was known to everyone as the gentle giant. During the Gulf War, his SEAL Team had performed superhuman feats of heroism. After being attacked and pinned down with three wounded warriors, Duffy had repelled countless attacks until relieved. During the heaviest fighting, he had crawled over thirty yards, under heavy fire, to drag a wounded soldier to safety and bind his critical wounds. The soldier was a seventeen-year-old Iraqi boy. He had risked his life to save an enemy combatant.

Duffy, like the other two men, had listened intently as Joe asked good, intelligent questions and in return all had given him invaluable advice.

Joe made it his mission, his quest, to search out extraordinary men of valor, listen to their stories, and seek their counsel.

It was ten days before Christmas when Lizzie answered the phone:

"Please, Mom, don't say anything; just listen. I will be away for several months and won't be able to call, and I know how you worry. I promise I'll be fine and will see you before you know it. Forgive me for missing Christmas, but I put a couple of things in the mail for you and Dad."

It took all her strength but Lizzie held her tears and pushed her broken heart aside to encourage her son.

"Oh, honey, you're the smartest guy I know, and it won't take long. Shake those jumping beans outt'a your pants, come on home, and give your mama a hug. Tell me where I can send you some money and it'll just be between you and me."

Joe told her he had saved plenty of money and he would call again as soon as he could. The following morning, Joe enlisted in the military as a tactical linguist and, as very few could, intended to become a US Army Ranger.

Plans, they say, are like intentions—everything looks better on paper. His ASFAB scores were so abnormally high they were double-checked by a US Army major who oversaw such things. At 6'2", 185 pounds, and a chiseled body, Joe went through the medical without incident. That is, discounting the flirtation by a young Navy flight surgeon named Amy. She looked at his chart again and then leaned close to his ear.

"Joseph Chandler, if you get back to San Diego I'd be happy to give you a more thorough exam."

Joe stared at the floor until he was rescued by a US Navy lieutenant commander. The officer pulled him into a small room and closed the door.

"Young man, you are too smart and way too educated to join the Army. If your heart is set on Special Forces or Combat Infantry, at least consider the Navy Seals. However, I would be remiss if I didn't tell you—you would make an exceptional line officer or, better yet, a Navy pilot. Please reconsider your decision."

Joe looked at the wings on the man's chest, thanked him, and thirty minutes later, Joseph Daniel Chandler was sworn into the US Army. An Army major had also taken his best shot at Joe, offering an immediate slot in Officer Candidate School, but to no avail.

In less than a week, Joe received orders to join a company of his fellow recruits, on the second day of January, at Fort Benning, Georgia.

By March, he was bored and wondered how some of the young men would make it without their mamas. After graduation from basic, Joe was assigned to advanced training at the Defense Language Institute in Monterey, California, where he also excelled. His assigned language was Modern Standard Arabic, and he graduated first in his class. The following day, Joe received his orders from a lieutenant colonel.

"Specialist, you have been granted a gift and I hope you don't disappoint me. With the combination of your academic and physical agility scores, I have recommended you for RASP, the Ranger Assessment and Selection Program at Fort Benning. Now you go out there and give 'em hell, Chandler."

"Thank you, sir. I won't let you down."

"No, Specialist, I suspect you won't. You're dismissed."

After completing airborne training and his RASP-1 assessment, Joe adorned his tan beret and joined an elite group of soldiers. It was neither expedient nor necessary for him to move on to the last phase—Ranger School. For the time being, he would serve in the 75th Regimental Special Troops Battalion, or the RSTB. The special battalion was formed for soldiers such as intelligence specialist, medics and linguists to provide critical support roles to US Army Rangers. The following morning, Joe was invited to the office of Col. John Paul Kelly, the commanding officer for the 75th RSTB.

"At ease, Chandler. Looking at your performance assessment, you just might make a damn fine soldier. If you had the time in service and a little more experience, I'd send you directly on to Ranger School, but what we need right now are men with your support skills. Specialist, I'm recommending you for immediate promotion to corporal and, once approved, you will be assigned to the 75th Rangers in Djibouti. Have you ever heard of it?"

"Yes, sir. Actually, I have: it's on the Horn of Africa and if I'm not mistaken, directly across the gulf from Yemen."

"That's right, Chandler. You are the only person I've met who knew that. Hell, I had to look it up myself. What else do you know about the region?"

"I know how important the Mandeb Straight is; it's the gateway to the Suez Canal. In Arabic, sir, it's called *Bab-El-Mandeb*, the Gate of Tears. Legend suggests it got its name from all the souls who lost their lives during an earthquake that divided the two continents. And, if I recall, sir, I believe French as well as Arabic is spoken there."

"That's impressive, Specialist, damned impressive. Didn't want to be an officer eh, Chandler?"

"No, sir."

"So not really thinking about a career in the Army I suppose?"

"I'm not sure, sir."

"Well, you should: we need more men like you. Okay, Chandler, you're probably smart enough to have already figured this out but pay attention anyway and maybe I'll go home tonight thinking I told you something you didn't know.

"Africa is a mess. While we had a momentary foothold with a few bases, it's getting damn hard to find a country who will house us. We have about 4,000 men and women at Camp Lemonnier in Djibouti, and we run a lot of Predator Drones out of there. Unfortunately, the neighborhood is getting crowded as China just signed a one-hundred-million-dollar-a-year rental contract with the Djibouti government. That, of course, is making this current administration very nervous. I probably don't have to tell you how much crude oil comes through those shipping lanes. Anyway, we have some Rangers over there right now and they could use your help. They need a good tactical linguist and I think you're just the man for the job. You're dismissed, Specialist, and good luck."

For the entirety of his first deployment, Joe supported his team in a variety of Eastern African countries. While the 75th Rangers were in the region only to assist, train, and observe, there were thousands of radicals in Ethiopia, Sudan, Somalia, and Yemen who would be happy to kill an American soldier. Perhaps the most interesting thing to observe was the ongoing construction of the large airstrip and naval base the Chinese denied they were building.

At the completion of his first tour of duty, a US Army captain by the name of Johnson asked Joe to join him for a libation. The captain had just arrived to relieve the previous unit commander.

"Corporal, it's not my call but it is my prerogative to ask, so I will. Word has it that you are an invaluable asset over here. I know you've done your time but if for any reason you wished to volunteer for a second deployment in this lovely piece of the world, I would not object. As you know, I'm the new guy and I could sure use your experience."

Joe liked the new captain already more than his predecessor, so Joe told him he would certainly give it some thought. That is, after his thirty days of leave.

Even Drummer seemed to be in good spirits and, of course, Lizzie fussed and doted over Joe and cooked all his favorite dishes. There were parties and reunions galore until Joe asked for a reprieve.

"Actually, if no one objects I'd like to help with some pruning and ride the tractor for a few days."

He and his father took long walks and talked about wine, farming, and a little of Africa. Since Lizzie had threatened him, Drummer made every effort to mend the relationship, which wasn't a difficult task, and it pained him to say goodbye.

CHAPTER 4

CIA 101

Afghanistan

Joe did volunteer for another deployment in Africa and the captain was fortunate to have him. During a routine scouting patrol across the border in Somalia, a poorly organized pocket of Al-Shabaab, a regional Islamic terror group, ambushed his team. After pulling the wounded captain from certain death, Joe returned fire and called in air support, including a medevac chopper for the captain. As the Black Hawk was landing, Corporal Chandler killed two Islamic fighters attempting a self-propelled-grenade attack on the helicopter. As fate would have it, the incident occurred thirteen days before the end of his second tour. Joe had deployed two years earlier as a tactical linguist and was on his way home as a decorated sergeant. For his actions of bravery under fire, Joe received a unit citation ribbon and was awarded the Bronze Star.

After a week with friends and family, Joe put a set of plugs and a new fuel filter in his 1958 Chevy Impala convertible and drove down the coast of California. After a brief stop in Monterey and having a beer with Duffy in Coronado, he took the scenic route east and returned to his unit at Fort Benning, Georgia.

When Sergeant Chandler reported to the 75th Regimental Special Troops Battalion, there was a notice for him to call and make an appointment with his regimental commander. Two days later, he walked into the office of Col. Moses Andres who had replaced Col. John Paul Kelly, now a one-star general at the Pentagon.

He waited outside the office until he was summoned by a clerk to go inside. He popped to attention.

"Sir, Sergeant Joseph Chandler reporting as ordered, sir."

Besides Col. Andres, there was a USAF Lt. Col. Pike and another man, apparently a civilian, who was wearing a suit. Suits made soldiers nervous.

"Have a seat, young man," said Col. Andres.

"Would you like something to drink? I'd say you've earned it."

"No, thank you, sir. I'm fine."

"Well, you did a fine job, Chandler, and congratulations on your commendation and your promotion to sergeant. These two men came a long way to talk to you, Sergeant, so I'm going to turn the meeting over to them. This is strictly an informational briefing, so relax and let's hear what they have to say."

Looking up from a file, the man in the suit started the meeting.

"It appears you have the proper clearance, so we'll get right to it. There are some 400,000 acres of poppies in Afghanistan and about half of it is in the Zhari District, down in the Kandahar province. Most of Afghanistan's heroin makes its way into Russia or Europe, but more and more is finding its way across our southern borders.

"Afghanistan has been a political hot potato, which has been passed around by administrations since Carter. Fifteen pounds of poppy paste, the output of a typical acre family plot, sells for around $600. This is in a country where twenty-five cents buys bread for a day, so, as you can imagine, a good poppy crop puts food on the table for much of Afghanistan. Honestly, what most Afghans want is to be left alone and go merrily about their business of farming. Unfortunately, their pretty-little poppy flowers are wreaking havoc on the rest of the world. Heroin is killing thousands of Russians, destroying an entire generations of Europeans, and use in the US is up by twenty-five percent in the last four years. And, Sergeant, the real pisser is right now, we need the Afghans' help, so we have to look the other way. Their people get their daily bread while the rest of the world gets their daily dose, all so we can fight the war on terrorism. That's politics, Mr. Chandler. However, the Taliban has changed the political winds. While they used to burn the crops in the name of Allah, now they are buying them to fund their terror campaigns, and Sergeant, it appears Mexico is a big buyer. This is where we believe you may be able to help us. The bottom line, Mr. Chandler, is we want to use you and your team to find the Taliban-Mexico connection.

"We know the cartels are fighting each other for a bigger stake in the international world of the heroin trade. They have become so emboldened in these efforts the crime syndicates are sending ambassadors directly to the Taliban to negotiate arms and money for heroin. If we find the Taliban's opium suppliers, we believe it will lead us to the Taliban sellers and the Mexican buyers. In order to do that, we need to find out what the farmers know. If it were possible, we would also love to have a discussion with one of those Mexican buyers. Are you following me, Sergeant? And if so, do you think you could handle it?"

"Yes, sir. I follow you fine, but, as you implied, this is a thousand-year-old problem, and if you stop a few Mexicans from buying Afghan heroin, a dozen more will take their place and, honestly, sir, if not the Mexican cartels, then buyers from anyone of a dozen countries in Europe or Asia. I'll do what I'm ordered, sir, but I'm not sure I see the point … with all due respect … sir."

"Sergeant, my name is Lt. Col. Pike and I work at the NSA. It's a great point and I completely agree with you. However, the problem right now lies with the extremely wealthy cartels of Mexico and South America. With billions to spend, someone has gotten their hands on some dangerously sophisticated weapons, probably Russian, and they are trading it to the Taliban for opium. Some folks way above my pay grade want it stopped and they are on our asses and expect an operational plan on their desks very soon. We ran this mission by State who punted it to DEA who said it was a military matter. We had a three-star give it a quick look and he said, and I quote, '*Find some talent, maybe Special Forces, but I want someone smart-as-hell, maybe somebody from Intel but give them all the support they need and get it done.*'

"Sergeant Chandler, you're a Ranger, you're smart, you're a good field tactician, and we believe you can get the job done. Am I wrong?"

"No, sir. I won't let you down."

"Very good then, I'll use every intelligence resource at my disposal to support your mission. I will be your eyes and ears and if you need anything, I will make damn sure you get it. We believe this mission is important, so you'll have my full attention. Before you leave for Kandahar, we are going to bring you up to speed with current satellite imagery of the region and educate you on some of the local customs and such. I know you have an educational background in the Middle East, so some of this will be a recap, but you may find it helpful. Any more questions?"

"No, sir; not at this time."

"All right Chandler, you'll report to Fort Mead next week and we'll need to make sure you hit the floor running. As a matter of fact, if you're ready, you're welcome to fly back with me."

"Thank you, Colonel, but I drove my own car back from Oregon and, if it's not a problem, I'd prefer to not leave it here."

Joe never caught the name of the man in the suit, but having spent over two years working Intelligence, he figured he was most likely a spook from the CIA. At least he gave the impression of being mission-oriented and not some self-important lackey. He thought the same of Col. Pike, a man who was capable of getting things done and looking after his men. The last thing Joe wanted was to be a political pawn and get himself or others killed.

As they exited the building, Col. Pike saw Joe walk towards the '58 Chevy.

"Wow, Sergeant, what a beauty. Have you had her long?"

"Yes, sir. My dad found it in a barn around my sixteenth birthday and we restored it together."

"How about a ride someday? It'd be a walk down memory lane for me. I used to own a '57 but got stupid and sold it."

Joe tossed the keys to the colonel. "Just tell me what I'm driving and where I'm headed and I'll meet you there."

Pike threw Joe a set of keys and nodded towards an ugly US government-issued Ford Crown Victoria.

"Wow, nice ride, Colonel. I'll take good care of it."

"I'll get you a room for tonight and buy you dinner before I fly back. I gotta go show this to some old friends. I'll see you in an hour, sergeant."

It's not exactly what Joe had in mind but the smile on the colonel's face was worth the worry.

CHAPTER 5

THREE GUYS AND A GAL

Joe was a quick study and continued to impress everyone prepping him for the mission. Two weeks after his recruitment, he flew to Kandahar International Airport and reported to US Army Col. Omri Gunderson, commander of the 3rd Division, 75th Ranger Battalion.

"Come in, Sergeant, and have a seat. I have orders to get you over to the Zhari district. You know anything about it?"

"Only what I picked up at Ft. Mead and some personal research; I welcome anything you could add, sir."

"Well, in a nutshell most people in Zhari are ethnic Pashtuns. There are no less than a dozen tribes, the most prevalent of which are the Noorzai and Ghilzai. There are always nomads moving around and, of course, there's the Taliban. They have a long cultural history in the Zhari region, so we occasionally send some Rangers over there to support the NATO troops. Between the Taliban and the warlords, it's a nasty place. However, as I understand it, your being here has something to do with heroin. Chandler, I've got more people pulling at me than a Snickers bar at a Jenny Craig convention. Any chance you could give me the condensed version?"

"Yes, sir. Apparently, some of the Mexican drug cartels are fighting for control of the heroin trade. They need heroin and the Taliban needs money and weapons, and I plan to get in the middle of it, sir. I need to meet some poppy farmers and see who's doing business with the Taliban. We'd love to stumble onto one of their meet-and-greets and snag one of those cartel boys. Maybe we could figure out how they're getting arms to the Taliban. It's my understanding that some of those weapons are increasingly complicated. That's pretty much it, sir."

"That's a tall order, son, and I'll help you if I can, but like I said I'm busier than a dung beetle at a congressional fund raiser, so you and your team are going to have to improvise some."

"Yes, sir. I understand."

"All right then, there's a Forward Operating Base on the river near the town of Gereshk. It is primarily secured by NATO, but we have a small presence of Infantry and a few Rangers over there doing some training with the Afghan Army. You go see Lieutenant Lee when you land and he'll fix you up with a place to stay. Including yourself you'll have a five-man team, so I suggest you make sure somebody knows where you are at all times. You should be welcomed by most of the tribes, and with the doc I'm assigning to your team, you'll get through a few more doors. Lee said he cannot spare an interpreter right now, but the doc speaks pretty good Pashto. If there are no more questions, I have a Black Hawk headed there with supplies at 1500 hours. You got all your gear?"

"I'm good to go, sir."

The colonel yelled for his sergeant and had him drive Joe to the flight line, where he hopped aboard a Black Hawk helicopter and flew west.

After a short meeting with the lieutenant, Joe was introduced to Petty Officer Third Class Percival Davis, a Navy corpsman.

"I'm headed over to get some chow, so if you want to stow your gear, you can eat with me."

They walked to a barracks and into a small space Joe wouldn't have to share.

"I wasn't expecting my own room."

"You're the team leader, Sergeant, and the lieutenant says you get your own room. The way I see it, as long as you know what you're doing and don't get anyone killed, you can have the whole barracks."

The reality of leading men into harm's way hadn't hit him until that moment. It caused him to pause, but the corpsman broke his inflective mood.

"Everybody calls me Doc; I take pride in my job and you look like a guy who will be good at yours, now let's go eat."

As it turned out, the corpsman did know his trade well and had used it extensively in combat with the Marines. Davis had a passion for battlefield medicine and a knack for languages. It's not uncommon for the military to use its medical personnel to build relationships with the various tribes. The Pashtuns had little in the way of medical services and Doc Davis had enjoyed going into villages and engaging the locals. In doing so, he had learned some Dari and almost mastered Pashto. Once his unit headed home, he requested to stick around and had eventually found his way to Lieutenant Lee, mostly as an interpreter.

The rest of the team walked in together and Doc waved them over. Sparky Nussbaum was a communications specialist who was on his second deployment. Liam Greer was almost as new in the country as Joe was and had excelled at Ranger sniper school. Joe had to do a double take when Remi Sørensen introduced herself. She had a voice almost as small as she was, and at 5'2" she didn't cast much of a shadow. Corporal Sørensen was a Special Operations engineer with the Norwegian Army currently serving with NATO. She was short, quiet, and had left her boot marks over the backs of several men who had washed out. She had short blonde hair, freakishly blue eyes, and a modest smile.

"This is Remi Sørensen," said Doc. "She's so little she keeps getting overlooked, but word has it she can blow up an entire Taliban village with a stick of gum."

"Yeah," said Greer. "I could also use a spotter and she's small enough she might be a good asset, no objections from me."

Joe looked at Sparky Nussbaum who shrugged his shoulders and looked back at Remi. Joe stared at her for a second without saying anything then asked her to have a seat.

"Ms. Sørensen, we're not going to blow up any villages, but we are going to be dangerously exposed to some nasty people. No one here knows anything about our mission, so at the moment I'll take your place on this team under advisement. As soon as I figure out where, plan on a briefing at 0700 tomorrow. After the general outline and before I get into specifics, if anyone wants out I'll need you to do so immediately."

Joe grabbed his tray, nodded at everyone, and walked away. He wanted the team to have time to think and talk among themselves. It was a classic move, and it left little doubt in anyone's mind as to who was in charge. Joe walked directly to Lieutenant Lee's trailer and stepped inside.

"I figured you'd be back, Sergeant. You want the low-down on your team, especially the sixteen-year-old-looking blonde, right?"

Joe smiled and nodded.

"All right, here's the deal: I got a call from Colonel Gunderson who told me he had some stout brass up his ass about this mission of yours. He said to give you the best I could spare.

"Sparky is a top-notch soldier, but he's got a little attitude. He's not excited about the assignment, and he would like to ride out his second deployment without too much drama. You can probably count on him, but he'll be high maintenance.

"Liam Greer is the best shooter I've ever seen. He's a bit green, but if you build some confidence in him, I think he'll be reliable.

"The Doc is as good as they come. He is an excellent field medic, good linguist, and the tribal folks like him. He's delivered babies, pulled teeth, and, amazingly, did an emergency appendectomy in the middle of nowhere. By far, he'll be your best asset in the field."

"And the girl?" asked Joe.

"The girl is Gunderson's idea. We don't know what else to do with her and she's eager to get out of the camp. Her sergeant said he's scared of her, and her file is chalked full of commendations. I guess she's smart, tough as nails, and follows orders. It'll be your call but, as I said, the colonel thought it was a good idea. Welcome to Afghanistan."

Joe nodded and thanked him, then asked where he could do a briefing the next morning.

"I'll have my first sergeant show you to a trailer we use for briefings. I'll make sure you're not interrupted unless we start taking mortar fire again."

Joe squinted his eyes and gave him an *Are you kidding?* look.

"It happens, so keep your helmet on."

Joe took a walk around the compound ... with his helmet on, thought about everything the lieutenant had said, then he invited the Doc for a chat.

There was some small talk about where they were from and what they planned to do once all the excitement was over. When the conversation died down, Joe stared at Doc Davis.

"Yeah," said Doc. "I think Remi will be fine. I think she's bright, pays attention, and will do whatever is asked of her. She's already followed me into the field a couple of times and I was glad to have her. She picks things up quickly, you know what I mean?"

"And what about Nussbaum?"

"Yeah, like I said, she picks things up quickly. She could probably learn to use a radio."

Joe ate breakfast alone while he read an illegally obtained personnel file on Remi Sørensen. His NSA connections were already paying dividends. The colonel's recommendation or not, it was his team, his call, and he didn't want to get anybody killed. At 0659, he walked into the modular trailer where everyone else was seated around a table.

"The Taliban is buying opium from a few poppy farms and either selling it or trading it to Mexican drug cartels for weapons. Some of those weapons are a problem. The cartels are desperate for heroin; so desperate, in fact, they are sending people to meet and negotiate with the Taliban. Our mission is to find the farmers, identify the buyers, and, with any luck, grab a Taliban seller *and* a Mexican buyer and turn them over for interrogation."

"It's a hell of a lot easier to kill the bastards than try and capture them, don't you think, Sergeant?"

Joe looked at Sparky Nussbaum then turned to Remi Sørensen.

"Ms. Sørensen, what do you think?"

"I think the intel is better when they are alive, sir."

"Ms. Sørensen, my name is Joe. I am not an officer, so it's just Joe *or* Sergeant, but not 'sir.' Another question, Ms. Sørensen: what do—"

"Excuse me, Sergeant, but it's Remi, Corporal, or Sørensen if you prefer, but *Ms. Sørensen* is my mother."

"Duly noted, Corporal. Now, as I was going to say, do you have any experience with communications equipment?"

"I do actually, quite a bit."

"Okay, last question: do you think Mr. Nussbaum should be on this team?"

Both Doc and Liam looked at Remi and then at Sparky. Sparky's mouth was open and he looked like a jock who saw his girlfriend kiss the class geek.

Doc and Liam jerked their heads back to Remi, who looked Sparky directly in the eyes.

"I think Corporal Nussbaum should sit this one out, Sergeant."

All eyes shifted to Sparky, who looked shocked and pissed.

"Yeah, that's what I think as well, Remi. Corporal, you're dismissed."

Sparky had a smirk on his face when he grabbed his helmet and headed for the door. He reached for the handle, turned to the group who was still staring at him.

"I'll grab my gear; I think I'll find another place to sleep."

When Joe turned to face his team, everyone was smiling.

"Look, folks, this is not going to be easy but it's very important. Anyone with reservations—now is your chance."

All eyes were on Joe and everyone was still smiling.

"Liam, I want you three hundred yards out, and Remi, I want you spotting for Liam. Remi, you said you had communication experience. Can you clarify?"

"I had a seven-day class on blowing up satellite and radio equipment. It's best if you get the antennas first."

Joe looked at Doc, who's smile had faded and was shaking his head.

"Want me to go get Sparky?" asked Doc.

"Remi, do you have any actual experience at calling in positions, air strikes, or equipping a team with wireless coms?"

"I do not, Sergeant, but by the time we leave I'll be an expert. No worries."

Joe exhaled and looked at Liam and Doc.

"All right then; as I was saying, Remi, you spot for Liam and handle coms. Doc and I will wear wireless earbuds and be dependent on you for fluid intel. Got it?"

Liam looked at Remi who nodded then said, "No problem whatsoever, Sergeant."

"Doc, we'll go in and see if we can make friends, check their blood pressure, and ask a few questions. If we find the right sort, someone who hates the Taliban, maybe we'll get lucky."

Joe looked at each of them, trying to find doubt or reservation, and saw neither.

"Once we actually identify a viable target and this thing gets real, we'll have either drone or satellite support from the NSA. Remi, you'll be getting real-time directions from a controller who will be able to see everything that moves. The important thing is not to panic and keep us updated.

"Last thing: if we are blindsided or find ourselves in a compromised situation—Liam, you'll have to make the call. Take as many shots as you can, then take Remi and get out. Are there any questions? All right then, let's go get some chow and I'll get an intel update and try to put together a timeline."

Doc and Liam walked out and Remi caught Joe by the arm.

"I will not let you down, Sergeant."

"It never crossed my mind, Corporal. We're lucky to have you. Get something to eat and let me talk to Lee and see who the communications guru on the base is."

"If you don't mind, Sergeant, I'll take care of it."

"All right, Sørensen, your show; just get it done."

For the next five days, everyone was busy. Joe, Liam, and Doc were looking at maps and intel reports; every other day, Remi would take a break from her training and check in. When Joe asked how it was going, she said she found the best com guy on base and was learning everything possible. The wireless earpieces had just arrived from Kandahar so she took the opportunity to fit Joe and the Doc. She spotted for Liam every time he went to shoot, and watched real-time satellite footage and could not believe the clarity of the men moving along the road—all from a camera mounted to a drone at 12,000 feet.

On Saturday afternoon, Colonel Pike gave Joe the intel he needed and the coordinates for two poppy farms. Joe called the team together and told them they would be heading out early Sunday morning. Everyone thought the team was ready. It was pizza and movie night, so the plan was to meet there. Joe asked Remi to stay for a second after the meeting.

"I never had a chance to ask about your communications tutor. It sounds like you had someone very good."

Remi looked at Joe and smiled. "Did you always know?"

"It's an important mission, Remi; it's my job to know."

"When I first got here, I couldn't catch a break. I joined the Army to make a difference; I wanted to fight. I've always had to prove myself because I'm a girl, and because I'm short. I am the baby of seven kids and the first six were boys. I could whip two of them by the time I was twelve and two others were afraid of me. When I finally deployed to a FOB, I was continually passed over for patrols and opportunities to engage the Taliban. It's actually worse in the International Security Force than the Norwegian Army; no one wants to get the little girl killed. Anyway, Sparky saw my frustration and came to my rescue. He got me on a couple of patrols with him, then a few with Doc. Sparky and I flirted a little and I even kissed him goodnight once. You know, it gets lonely out here but nothing else happened, if you know what I mean. He didn't have anything to do with me getting this assignment, and in fact it pissed him off. I found out about your mission from Sparky, then hitched a ride to HQ and personally asked Col. Gunderson for a break. Sparky said it was probably a suicide mission and neither of us should have anything to do with it. He didn't actually know I was on the team until I showed up at the mess hall."

"How in the heck, Remi, did you get his help to train you after you threw him under the bus; he had to have felt betrayed?"

"It was easy, Sergeant, I just asked him. He knows I told the truth. It embarrassed him, but he and I both knew his heart wasn't in the mission. He had a very difficult first deployment and lost two good friends in Iraq. He's the very best at his job but he hates this war, and he wants to go home. When I explained how dangerous it was for the rest of the team, he agreed. He also knew how badly I *did* want to be on the team. It's the opportunity I've been waiting for, so he agreed; no one could do a better job at training me than Sparky."

"That is an amazing story, Corporal, and I'm glad it all worked out. I don't have any regrets about booting him from the team, but he sounds like a stand-up guy."

"He's okay, Joe, but he had no business on this mission. Now how about some pizza?"

CHAPTER 6

DIVA

Mel Randle woke early and surprisingly refreshed from her evening at Segundo Vida. The previous day had begun with caution and common sense thrown to the wind, as she had taken on three different hot coffees drinks—one double shot, iced caramel macchiato, plus a sundry of homemade baked delights. Fortunately the handsome barista had rescued her from herself, and treated her to an unforgettable evening where she had learned volumes about his family and disclosed almost nothing about herself. She wasn't hiding closely guarded secrets or ashamed of anything; it was the tremendous storm raging within that was scaring her to death. Mel had spent the last seven years of her life meticulously preparing for something, which, suddenly, she had little interest in or any passion to pursue.

Her family was, as they say on the dairy, *"going to have a cow."* This was especially true of her brother Peter Alan Randle, or Rand as everyone called him. Since they were kids, he had been her closest friend and biggest supporter. Her dad would hear her out, shake his head in a Swedish kind-of-way, then slowly walk off toward the calving stalls. Her mom would cry, pray, and trust Jesus but Rand—oh my God, Rand was going to confront her, reason with her, then totally freak out. In the meantime, what Mel needed was a comforting quad shot of espresso hidden beneath a dense blanket of steamed whole milk. Afterward she needed a friend, and the closest thing she had was a virtual stranger called Gringo Joe.

She slipped into her favorite pair of faded blue jeans, a comfortable tee shirt, and an extremely old and well-worn SF Giants ball cap. It was still foggy outside, so she also threw on her Stanford hoodie and started walking toward the heavenly aroma of cinnamon and freshly roasted coffee beans. Mel was used to spending time alone and had always been cautious and observant, extremely aware of her surroundings. This morning, what caught her eye, was a Hispanic man hunched down in his nondescript white van across from the shop. She would have let it pass but, unmistakably, she had seen a camera with a telephoto lens pointed toward Joe's. Once the man saw her, he lowered the camera and looked away. She kept her eyes forward, pulled her hoodie over her ball cap, and started grooving to music that wasn't playing.

"*Sólo otro niño perezoso Americano.* Just another lazy American kid," he mumbled before starting his van and driving away.

"Good morning!" said a perky bleach-blonde girl with a full sleeve of tats on her left arm.

"Good morning," Mel replied.

"Is Joe around? He said he was opening this morning."

"Oh! You must be the reason," she replied.

"Ahhh ... the reason?" quipped Mel with a slight tinge of rawness to her voice.

"Hey, someone needs her happy drink. No disrespect intended there, girly girl. It's only because Joe had such a spring in his step and was whistling this morning. Heck, I figured he got lucky last night, but I should have known better. I swear the man is a closet priest or something, but have you ever laid eyes on such a hunk ... I'm just say'n."

Still chewing on the "girly girl" comment, Mel decided a quad shot might be the tipping point, so to save Ms. Perky an ass-whipping, she dialed it back a bit and ordered a tall two-shot vanilla latte, paid, and took a seat by the window. In no time at all, Ms. Perky bounced over with her coffee, just as a couple walked in.

"Hey, Diva," said the woman, as her significant other showed a toothy grin.

"Hey, girly girl," she replied.

"Will it be the usual for you two?"

"Of course, but make it to go. Where's Joe?"

"Oh, he rushed out of here a few minutes ago. He does that all the time. I swear he probably went to hear a confession or something."

The couple laughed, as if getting an inside joke.

"Yep," the woman said.

"I've tried to set that hunk up a dozen times with my cousin, Louise, but he'll have none of it. I swear I daydream about him myself."

"I'm right here, honey."

"Just kidding, sweetie. You know I got eyes for nobody but you, pumpkin."

Everyone laughed and even Mel had to hide a grin. After the couple left, in no time at all, Diva walked over with a warm marionberry scone.

"On the house," she said.

"It takes folks a time or two to get me but I swear, girly girl, I'll grow on you."

Mel looked at the plate and then back at Diva.

"Girly girl, you had me at the scone."

They both giggled, and then the two indulged in some shallow banter about the community of Steelhead.

"It's darn near impossible to find a single man around here who has all his teeth, a job, and don't still live with his mama."

Mel told Diva she had traveled extensively and assured her it wasn't a problem exclusive to Steelhead, Oregon.

"It seemed to have happened when I was in college. It was like something in the universe broke and all at once men stopped being men. They all began playing video games and moved back in with their parents. I swear, by my sophomore year in college, girls couldn't get a date unless they played *Halo* or *League of Legends*."

"Girly girl I hear ya, but I'm just say'n, I love that you've seen all those places and done so many things—and college, my goodness! I thought about beauty school but Joe talked me out of it. He has me gettin' my GED and pays me real good. I pick on him, but I swear they broke the mold with that one. And, girly girl, if you don't know it yet, his folks got more money than the governor."

A door slammed in a back room and Joe walked in looking a bit disheveled but still better than most.

"Hello," he said.

"Wasn't sure I'd see you again."

"Hello yourself. You get a girl hooked on caffeine and sugar and you expect her to run off and get treatments elsewhere?"

"Well, it just so happens we do offer a rehab program right here for the low, low price of nineteen ninety-nine."

They both laughed as Joe excused himself and headed for several customers patiently waiting for his coveted attention. Diva started making drinks and Mel caught up on a few emails. She scrolled through them but tried to ignore the ones from several law firms asking her to finalize an interview. Of course, there were about a dozen texts from her brother. Mel walked out front, sat on a comfortable bench, and called her mom. It was going well but when her mom mentioned that her dad and Rand were worried about her, she almost cried.

"Everything is okay—right, honey? I mean we are all so proud of you and can't wait until you land a big job and find yourself a nice boy to marry."

"Listen, Mom. I have a few things to work through before I... before I... well, do something I may regret. I know it sounds uncharacteristic but I need a few more weeks. I love you all and I'll be in touch—okay, Mom?"

"Okay, honey, but we sure are worried about you, so you let us know if there is anything wrong. And you know your daddy will walk over hot coals for his little girl."

"I know, Mom, and I'm fine... really. Besides, I did meet a nice boy. You'd both like him. I have to go, Mom. I love you."

As soon as she hung up, she stomped her foot and clenched her teeth.

"Oh, my God," then she screeched irritably to herself. "Did I really just tell my mom I met a nice boy?"

Of course she was shamelessly appeasing her mother, and it was a spur-of-the-moment remark, but still.

"Oh-my-God!" she said again, this time a bit louder.

"Are you all right?"

Mel jumped and almost took a swing at Joe who was looking at her with substantial concern. Before her filters kicked in, Mel said, "No! No, I'm not all right. And why would a man hiding in a van be taking pictures of your coffee shop?"

Joe reached out and put his hand on her shoulder. "What if we take a drive out to the vineyard? It's where I do my best listening and, right now, I think you desperately need to talk. What do you say, Mel? Will you trust me?"

She had to turn away before he saw her eyes puddle. "I could use a friend right now, Joe, but I really don't want to be a bother."

They said goodbye to Diva who warned Joe to be on his best behavior.

"I like you, girly girl. Let's talk again, okay?"

Mel smiled, hugged her goodbye, then insisted they swing by the studio apartment so she could freshen up. They drove the seven miles and were about to pull into Segundo Vida when a nondescript white van passed them slowly, headed back into town.

"Hey! That's the—"

But before she could finish, Joe quickly and coolly said, "Eyes forward, Mel, and don't turn around."

Once they parked, Mel looked at Joe.

"Perhaps we both have some talking to do."

Drummer was down in California on business, so they said hello to Lizzie who insisted they have some quiche, fresh out of the oven. They shared a little vineyard gossip with his mom then retired to a very rustic office Joe had started building years earlier. It was located in the loft of a barn, which once served as storage for old wine barrels. At the top of the stairs, Mel saw the same craftsman style as the coffee shop. There was an antique desk, two red leather chairs, and some built-in shelves full of hardback and leather-bound books. She glanced at the titles and saw a lot of stuff about religion and history. There were three original painting on the walls; all exhibited the vibrant colors and festive people of Latin America. However, it was the photographs that caught Mel's eye. There was one of a man playing a guitar and a beautiful woman singing with him.

"That's Jose and Sonata," said Joe, watching carefully as she snooped around.

Mel smiled and moved on to a large photograph of Joe. He was standing next to some children in what appeared to be Mexico or Central America. Then there was a picture of him in his Army Ranger uniform, standing next to a very beautiful Hispanic woman.

"Wow! She's really pretty, and I had no idea you had been in the military." Mel was dying to ask who she was and her relationship to Joe, but she let it pass. "You are so full of surprises."

Joe smiled and nodded.

"Why don't you have a seat, Mel, and let's talk about you for a change. And maybe we should start with all the anxiety you're trying so hard to disguise."

She flopped heavily into the chair and remembered what Diva has said about Joe taking confessions. Mel wasn't Catholic but she believed in God, and if a good confession would help, so be it.

She told Joe all about her upbringing, her parents, and her close relationship with her brother who was now a successful walnut grower and commodities broker in Central California. Mostly, she spoke of the expectations—the ones she had always bore from her dad and the weightier ones she had placed on herself.

"I was the valedictorian of my class and captain of the debate team. I lettered in track and, after six years of bruised ribs and a dislocated shoulder, I earned a black belt in judo. I graduated magna cum laude from Stanford, spent a hellish summer in Washington DC working as an intern, and then graduated with honors from Stanford Law School. I studied very little and passed the California bar quite easily. My law professors loved me, my peers hated me, most guys were intimidated by me, and now I'm being courted by some fairly impressive law firms."

Mel had been staring out the window, gazing toward the vineyard, never once looking at Joe. Finally, she exhaled and turned to face him.

"And?" said Joe.

"And now I'm pretty sure I'd rather work with Diva at the coffee shop than in some stuffy law firm whose arrogant partners will expect their new protégé to bill over sixty hours a week."

It was Joe's turn to exhale, and he did so rather loudly.

"Wow!" he said, staring into her anxious brown eyes. "You need to understand, Mel, I don't think you have the temperament or experience necessary for the fast-paced life of a barista."

They both enjoyed a hardy and much needed laugh.

"Mel, believe it or not I know a great deal about expectations and disappointing parents. I gave mine such a shock, I worried if they would ever talk to me again. However, parents get over stuff; it's what they do. It sounds like you have a great family, but it also sounds as if you've been hoeing the same row for so long there couldn't help but be expectations. Maybe no one, you included, stopped digging long enough to question what would happen once you got there. The way I see it, it doesn't matter if you went to Stanford Law or some industrial school to be a welder. If you wake up one day and decide you don't like welding, you can't spend the rest of your life being miserable. As they say, just because you spent a lot of money on an ugly hat doesn't mean you have to wear it forever."

They were both quiet for several minutes until Mel looked up with a somewhat serious glare.

"Joe, I got that ball cap after watching the Giants beat the Dodgers in the summer of 2005. Moses Alou and J.T. Snow hit back-to-back homers and my dad bought me that cap, and I never really thought of it as ugly—really worn, but not ugly."

Joe lost the color in his face and his mouth dropped open as he made a lame attempt to explain it was simply a metaphor. Mel started laughing.

"Gotcha!" she said. "That's payback for your insensitive barista remark."

"Oh, man! You definitely got me."

After another laugh, the mood steadied a bit and Mel told Joe how much she appreciated him listening.

"So, what are you going to do? If it's not being an attorney, have you thought about a different career?"

"It's not that I don't want to be an attorney per se. It's the idea of working for a corporate firm either suing someone or designing mergers that put good folks out of work. I'm still thinking about it but whatever it is, it needs to be challenging and it's got to be fun."

"Great idea," said Joe. "And I can't think of a better place to figure things out than a sleepy little town in rural Oregon. Which reminds me, about that dinner at the mayors—are you interested?"

"Why not?" she said. "How could I pass on the opportunity to appear in public with Steelhead's most eligible bachelor and disappoint all those hopeful matchmakers?"

That seemed to embarrass Joe a little but Mel didn't mind a bit.

"If you're sure you're all right, I should get back and give Diva a break. I told her I would close tonight. Hope you don't mind."

They walked down the stairs together to find Jose waiting for an opportunity to speak with Joe. When Joe introduced the two, Mel was caught off guard by Jose.

"You are not only a beautiful lady," he said. "You must be very special. This *cabeza de calabaza*—oh, I am sorry, it means pumpkin head—he never brings the girl here ... sometimes, I wonder ... you know ... maybe he *loco*."

Joe looked at his shoes and Mel smiled, then took her cue and told them she needed to make a call.

"*Lo siento mi amigo.* I do not mean to interrupt."

"You are never an interruption, Joe. What's on your mind?"

"Well, amigo. I saw the van again. I think this man is Mexican and maybe dangerous, no?"

"Perhaps he is, but regardless, keep your eyes open and call me if he shows up again—okay, my friend?"

The two men hugged and did the manly backslap thing and Joe walked to his car.

"It was cold and foggy this morning, and now it's so beautiful. Just look at those fluffy clouds and these beautiful rolling hills. I think you're right, maybe it's not a bad place to sort things out."

CHAPTER 7

Poppycock, Peekaboo, and the Posse

Joe had requested and been granted five days of R&R for his team at Bagram AFB, in the Parwan Province of Afghanistan. In the last sixteen weeks, they had been in four different provinces and seven districts of Afghanistan. They had flown, driven, and walked a thousand miles, talked to dozens of poppy growers and tribal leaders, and they were tired and frustrated. The intel always looked good and prospects bright, but after the last dead end, Joe's team was beginning to feel it had all been for naught. They took long hot showers and decided to take a break from each other. There was a movie theatre, a bowling alley, and numerous fast food restaurants. At eight o'clock, on his second night there, Joe walked into a pizza parlor for a late dinner and a cold beer. He placed his order, grabbed his Budweiser, and turned around to see three familiar faces smiling back at him. Liam, Doc, and Remi lifted their mugs and in unison yelled, "Cheers!"

As he took his seat, he looked around and smiled.

"Well, truth is I was wondering where you guys might be."

"What's next, Joe?" asked Liam.

"I have a teleconference with NSA tomorrow morning and I'm going to ask the same thing. I feel like their intel is either late, wrong, or we're chasing ghosts."

"I figure words out," said Doc. "We've covered a lot of ground, talked to enough people, and you have to believe the Taliban knows we're looking. I think if something doesn't break for us soon, we're either going to get set up and killed, or continue to be the brunt of their jokes. Sometimes I picture the tribal leaders laughing at us around their campfires."

"What do you think, Remi?" asked Liam.

"I like to bowl," she replied.

They finished off Joe's pizza and got in thirty frames before calling it quits and losing five bucks each to Remi.

It had been a while since Joe had spoken to Colonel Pike, much less seen his face.

"How's your team holding up, Chandler?"

"We're fine, Colonel; we needed a break but everyone's healthy."

"That's good to hear because I need you packed and ready to head out first thing tomorrow. I know it's not what you want to hear, but we have some good intel and I want you to move on it."

Joe had heard the same thing from the districts of Panjwayi, Khanashin, Washir, and several more he couldn't remember.

"It's good intel, Chandler; you need to move on this one."

Joe exhaled slowly and asked the colonel what he had.

"We intercepted a cell phone conversation about a meeting in the Arghandab Valley two days from now. It was placed to an office in Kandahar, and the cell was a burner purchased in Tijuana, Mexico. We believe it's reliable and we definitely want to move on it. Any questions?"

"Arghandab Valley—that's back down in the Zhari District, sir?"

"We always thought Helmand and Kandahar were our best chances, but we just haven't caught a break. Look, I know you must be frustrated but let's check it out and hope for the best. I'll find your team a ride back down to Kandahar and we'll talk again tomorrow night. Pike out."

Joe found his team and gave them the good news, and they were just as excited as he was.

Pike and Joe talked again and pinned down the coordinates of the farm. It bordered a river on its south side and butted up to a very small village to the west. Once Joe looked at it on a map, he realized he had been there and had probably been jerked around by the owner. Abdul-Ali was the tribal chief of the Ghilji, the dominant tribe in the district, and owned this particular twenty-acre poppy farm. Joe didn't like him the first time they met, and knew the feeling was mutual. When they had walked away, Doc said he smelled like Taliban.

The mission was dubbed Poppycock; during communications, the NSA was Peekaboo, and Joe's team was duly named the Posse. The small village was on the north side of the Arghandab River where, on the previous night, Joe and Doc had taken position inside an empty goat hut. Liam and Remi were across the river, dug in and well-camouflaged at 750 meters. The village made a semicircle facing the river, giving them a broad view of each hut. Three kilometers behind Liam and Remi was a road where a Humvee had dropped the team and left them to walk. The meeting was scheduled for 10:00 AM, but at 09:30 the powerful Aegis camera, mounted to the Predator drone hovering at 12,000 feet, was picking up no activity. At 09:40, that all changed.

"Posse this is Peekaboo, do you copy?"

"Roger that, Peekaboo, you are crystal clear," responded Remi.

"Posse, please be advised you have two inbound vehicles. One is a truck, six kilometers out, carrying two armed men in the back. We cannot confirm passengers inside, copy?"

"Roger that, Peekaboo—one truck, three confirmed. Do you have an ETA, over?"

"Peekaboo estimates arrival time of vehicle number one to be five minutes. Second vehicle is a sedan with two confirmed. ETA is ten minutes. Do you copy?"

"Roger, Peekaboo. Please stand by."

"Joe, you have two vehicles inbound—number one is a truck with at least three confirmed, ETA is five minutes. Number two is a sedan with two confirmed, ETA ten minutes. Do you copy?"

"Affirmative," said Joe. "Notify the Calvary."

The Calvary referred to a UH-60 Black Hawk standing by at a small FOB only thirty klicks to the west.

"Roger that. Calvary is hot on the pad."

"Peekaboo, the Posse requests fluid updates, over."

"Affirmative, Posse. We are all eyes."

Everyone could see the dust from the incoming truck less than 1000 meters away. Suddenly, a door opened and two armed men stepped out of a small building. They had long beards and looked very much like Taliban.

"Where the hell did they come from?" whispered Doc.

Joe responded by shaking his head. When the truck entered the center of the small village, the two men in the back jumped out and intently looked around. One said something to one of the men who had come out of the building; the man shook his head no. Then the passenger door of the truck opened and a small man wearing the traditional black garments of the Taliban stepped out. The man said nothing but looked very nervous as he surveyed the buildings. When he finally spoke, the two gunmen from the truck moved into the shadows and the others went inside the building.

In less than two minutes, they could see the dust from the approaching sedan. Underneath the thick layer of Afghan dirt, it appeared to be the remains of what had once been a Mercedes 300 Diesel. Once it came to a stop, an older man with a big smile and arms flailing got out from behind the steering wheel.

"Well, I'll be…," whispered Joe, who was looking through his binoculars.

"Isn't that our resident tribal chief, Abdul-Ali?"

"I can't believe it," whispered Doc.

The two waited patiently to see what would happen next. When the rear door of the vehicle opened, a Hispanic man wearing dark sunglasses and a natural silk sports coat emerged. He looked as though he might piss his pants at any moment. The door of the building opened slightly and an arm extended and waved the Mexican inside. When the chief tried to enter, the door slammed in his face. He muttered something about someone's mother and a goat, and then walked into a small hut, sitting on stilts.

"Remi, can Liam see the two men outside, over?"

"Affirmative, clear line of fire."

"Okay, get the Calvary airborne. I don't think this will take long, out."

"Posse, you have two children approaching the goat pen, over."

"Roger that, Peekaboo, I see them."

"Joe, you have company in thirty seconds—two children."

Two young boys came around the corner, laughing with sticks in their hands. Just inside the goat pen, one stopped to pee while the other pointed and laughed at his penis. Just as they were about to come face-to-face with two Americans, a woman yelled from another cracked door. One of the boys cursed the woman and the other laughed and clasped his hand over his mouth, but both turned and headed up the dusty path.

Joe and Doc finally exhaled and looked back toward the houses. Soon, a door opened and a large woman with a *niqab* —a commonly worn veil over her face—stepped onto the porch, slapped one of the young boys on his ear, then dragged both inside and slammed the door. It appeared that several of the men from the tribe were out working in the fields, and the women were very uncomfortable with the presence of the unpredictable Taliban. Again, Remi's satellite phone crackled.

"Posse, this is the Calvary. We're fifteen klicks out, please advise."

Remi relayed the info to Joe who asked that they hold their location and stand by.

"Remi, this is about to get hot. Advise Liam that we want the Mexican and the chief alive; all others are targets. Do you copy?"

"Roger that."

Joe turned to Doc, who had his HK416 aimed down the road.

"Keep your eyes open and cover me. I'm going to the back of those buildings."

Doc nodded and looked back through his scope.

"Remi: as soon as anyone steps out of that building, call in the Calvary and tell them to hover right above us. Advise that there are women and children in the buildings. When everyone is out, Liam has a green light, do you copy?"

"Roger that."

Joe crawled out the back of the hut and ran around to the rear of the buildings, where no one on his team could see him. The meeting was in the third house down. As Joe crouched and made his way slowly past the first, a woman opened the back door of the second. She was holding a large bowl of some kind of liquid, which she heaved in Joe's direction. When her eyes came up, she found herself staring at an American soldier, and she froze. Joe put his finger to his lips and walked directly to her. She wore a hijab but no veil. Her eyes were wide and she never took them off him. He herded her inside, being careful not to touch her, and then he closed the door. He pointed to the front and motioned for her to move. All Joe wanted to know was who else was in that house. There was a baby asleep on a blanket and the woman looked at her child, then at Joe, and began trembling. All Joe could do was to sign to her that he meant no harm. He reached down, picked up the sleeping baby and put it in her arms, then led her to the back where there was a small cookstove. He pointed to a corner and motioned for her to sit, and she did. Again, he put his fingers to his lips then went out the back door.

The same time as Joe reached the meeting house, he heard the front door open and men talking. He quietly cracked opened the rear door and watched as two men stood. The first was an older man who looked battle-hardened and dangerous. The other looked more like a drugstore clerk who was playing dress-up. He was young and barely able to sprout the customary beard. The Mexican and Taliban leader remained on the rug, where they appeared to be engaged in a rather heated negotiation—both speaking broken English. Finally the *haji* and the Mexican shook hands and stood. As they were about to exit, someone outside yelled and pointed to the sky.

That would be the Black Hawk, thought Joe.

The hard-ass-looking Taliban turned to go back inside just as his head exploded. There was another pop from Liam's sniper rifle; at the same time, the Black Hawk door gunner disintegrated a man pointing an AK47 in his direction. The Taliban leader, still inside, pulled a ten-inch knife from his belt and grabbed the Mexican by his hair. He screamed something about a traitor and yelled "Allahu Akbar!" as he pulled back his arm to slit the Mexican's throat. His eyes were afire with rage and his teeth clinched in hatred when the 5.56 round from Joe's HK entered his forehead. The knife fell to the ground and Joe took another step forward to kill the last Taliban fighter in the room. The Mexican had fallen into a fetal position on the rug when the laser sight from Joe's rifle found the last man's head. He was crouched in a corner, unarmed, and Joe could not believe his ears.

"Don't shoot me, dude! Oh, my God, please don't shoot me! I'm an American, bro ... please don't shoot."

"What the ... *American,* did you say you were an American?"

The young man put his hands over his ears and started freaking out, but Joe grabbed him by his collar and pulled him, face down, into the middle of the room. He put his boot on his back and forced him flat, next to the Mexican when Joe heard Remi yell his name.

"In here!" he yelled. "Clear! I'm in here!"

Remi, with water still dripping from her clothes, eased into the room and looked around. She was about to ask a question when they heard a three round burst of gunfire and a windshield explode. Both Remi and Joe whirled, dropped to a knee with guns up, as they heard Doc yell, "Clear!"

The driver of the truck had never gotten out ... and had been overlooked by everyone—everyone but Doc. The man grabbed a rifle from the floorboard and raised it to shoot Remi as she walked into the house. It had been a fatal decision.

On Joe's command, Remi radioed the Black Hawk to hover right above the river, keeping the M240 machine gun pointed toward the village, while they did a house-to-house search. Once Abdul-Ali, Bill—the American Jihadi—and the Mexican were all cuffed with zip ties, and the women and children were corralled by Remi, a second Black Hawk landed behind the building. Lieutenant Lee and five US Army Rangers hit the poppy fields. In about ten minutes, they walked in with a half dozen Afghan men who had been spotted by the first Black Hawk. They were hiding in the field, too afraid of the Taliban to try and protect their wives and children. One of the farmers hugged his wife—the one with the baby—then walked over and kicked Abdul-Ali in the ribs. Everyone watched and no one said a thing.

"It looks like your patience paid off, Sergeant. Nice job, but what do we have here?"

"Thank you, sir, but it was my team; their performance was extraordinary."

Joe walked over to the prisoners and rolled the American face-up with his boot.

"Lieutenant Lee, meet Jihadi Johnson. This is William Johnson, age nineteen, from Malibu Beach, California. He says his dad is Huey Johnson."

"Huey Johnson ... wait, you mean Huey Johnson the actor, hater of all things patriotic and American?"

"Apparently so, sir. I don't think the apple fell very far from the tree."

"All right, folks, let's load 'em up. Where do you want your prisoners, Chandler?"

"I have orders to get them to the air base at Kandahar, and sir, I request permission to take my team if you have no objections."

"Permission granted. Where are you headed next?"

"I'm not really sure about that, Lieutenant. With any luck—home."

"Well, listen, Chandler, I can always use a good man; let me know if you need a job."

Once the three prisoners were loaded and Joe, Doc, and Remi were aboard, the Black Hawk touched down just across the Arghandab River. Only Joe hopped out to help Liam load a backpack of ammo, a communication pack, a camo tarp, and his .50 caliber sniper rifle.

"Good shooting, Liam."

"I have to confess, Sergeant, I was fine until Remi grabbed her gun and left. I guess I got used to the extra set of eyes. I was sure afraid I'd miss something."

"Well, pal, you didn't miss a thing. Let's go."

Lt. Col. Gunderson was only one of several interested parties on the tarmac when the Black Hawk landed. Besides the six MPs waiting to escort the prisoners to a detention center, there was a suit, and this one had a name.

"Hell of a show, Sergeant; you made us all proud but I'd expect nothing less. Well done, soldier."

Joe nodded and turned to his team.

"Colonel, I believe you know Corporal Remi Sørensen, but I'd be honored to introduce you to the rest of my team."

The colonel nodded and smiled broadly.

"Sir, this is Specialist Liam Greer, sniper extraordinaire, and I believe you've heard of Petty Officer Third Class Doc Davis. Colonel, every one of these people performed heroically in the face of fire and saved lives today, mine included."

Gunderson looked each of them in the eye, shook their hands, and thanked them. As the prisoners were escorted away, a suit joined the group.

"Sergeant Chandler, I'd like you and your team to follow this gentleman into one of our briefing rooms and listen to what he has to say. I'll excuse myself but, again, you all did your units and countries proud today."

Joe called his team to attention; they saluted the colonel and turned to follow the suit.

"I know what you all did today and I can only imagine how exhausted you are, so I will make this brief. My name is Howard Anderson—Dr. Howard Anderson actually, but my Ph.D. is in a silly random field, so I had to go to work for the US government. I am currently the liaison between NATO and a foundation that I oversee, but it is important that you know that my job carries a great deal of weight and authority. With that said, I regret to be the bearer of bad news. Your mission today was extremely important, but it is now classified. I am afraid there will not be an awards ceremony or any well-deserved metals handed out. I personally want to apologize, but it is critical that neither the Taliban nor the Mexican drug cartels learn what happened today. We'll let them assume there was a disagreement that ended badly. The impact of your mission will most likely save hundreds of lives, which is why a citation of merit is being attached to each of your permanent service records. It is my sincere desire that each of you one day receives the recognition you deserve. Now, with that said, I'm afraid that we need to make this a bit more official, so another person will join you and you'll be asked to sign a few documents, then you can go celebrate together."

As Dr. Anderson walked out, Major Horst—from Belgium, serving with the International Security and Assistance Force—walked in with a file under his arm. He introduced himself, said things which sounded a great deal like threats, then had each of them sign some papers. He read an international confidentiality document, but what they all heard was "blah, blah, blah."

When he excused them, Joe stood and asked the major if he'd excused himself instead and let them have the room. Though he hesitated, he saw the determination in Joe's eyes and walked out.

Joe looked at each of them for a few moments before speaking.

"I am a soldier, just like you. I did not join this fight for glory or ribbons, but today I'll walk away with something more valuable. I do not care if another single soul ever knows what we did as long as we do not forget each other."

Doc was the first to respond. "I will not forget."

Liam was next, "I will not forget."

It was a longer pause for Remi, who tried to keep the tears out of her eyes. "Today I became a soldier, and I will never forget."

The other three stood, walked to where Joe was standing, and they joined arms and formed a tight circle. Joe spoke quietly, "The Lord bless you and keep you; the Lord make his face to shine upon you and be gracious to you; the Lord lift up his countenance upon you and give you peace."

In unison they all said "Amen" and walked away.

CHAPTER 8

SAN MIGUEL

On Highway 19, just four miles inside the US border with Mexico, is the town of San Miguel, Arizona. On the outskirts of the old village, you will find the Queen of Angels Mission built by Father Bonaventure Oblasser in 1913. It served as both a church and school and was constructed to educate the Papago Indians and spread the doctrine of Catholicism across the plains and mountains of the Sonora Desert. However, on a hot, dusty Sunday morning, more than fifteen police, county sheriff, border patrol, state troopers, and one Bureau of Indian Affairs vehicles were scattered across the parking lot. The FBI would be the last to arrive. They were all at the scene of a tragic and growing trend along the border. Inside an abandoned forty-foot tractor trailer were the bodies of sixteen girls, ranging from age thirteen to maybe as old as seventeen. They were all from Central America, in this instance, Guatemala, and each one had been murdered by a single gunshot to the head. That is, all but one, who was in shock, sitting in the back of an ambulance, shaking uncontrollably. Her name was Maria Perez and she had lived because her would-be assassin's gun misfired and jammed. She was the next in line to be shot, but when the man turned around looking for enough sunlight to fix his gun, she had quietly lain down among her dead friends. Very quickly and quietly she rubbed a spot of blood in the middle of her forehead, and with eyes wide open she held her breath and lay very still. The man unjammed his pistol, shot the remaining four girls, closed the door of the trailer, and Maria drew a deep breath, and went into shock as he drove away. Junior Hernandez, a young janitor at the mission, heard the pop of the pistol, and watched the Ford pickup leave the parking lot. His Honda Trail 90 was parked on the other side. Junior knew what trouble was and he was scared, but he found the courage to call the police.

Sometimes bodies were found locked in trailers, where they had died of starvation or dehydration, but the murder of these young, innocent girls was something new and extremely troubling. Smuggling women across the border to accommodate the burgeoning sex trafficking and slave trade business had grown exponentially. Some of the girls were enticed with money or promises of jobs but most were simply kidnapped from their rural villages, never to be seen or heard from again. These atrocities were carried out by systematic, well-funded, and ruthless organizations and, almost without fail, were associated with the drug cartels. The cartels were already seasoned smugglers, so young girls—and lately, young boys—were just one more commodity.

Sherriff Monroe Culpepper, a thirty-five-year veteran of the police force, stood at the crime scene shaking his head, considering early retirement.

"Eddie," he said to his senior deputy, "what in the Sam Hill has happened to humanity?"

Eddie, a deacon at the First Baptist Church of San Miguel, said, "Sherriff, humanity has been broken since the dawn of mankind. There are some sick folks in the world, but this here, this is just pure-dee-ole-evil and it scares the jeepers out of me. Yes sir, it scares the absolute jeepers out of me."

From her office in Washington DC, Arizona Congresswoman Dr. Sally Marshall read the news release twice, picked up the phone, and dialed a number of which very few were entitled.

Congresswoman Marshall was not only the tough, spitfire daughter of a Tucson cattle rancher, she was also a decorated Apache Helicopter pilot from Operation Iraqi Freedom. After leaving the military, she graduated from the University of Arizona College of Medicine, worked as an ER doctor until she ran for—and won a seat in—the Congress. Marshall was well thought of by her constituents and was quickly appointed to a coveted position on the Permanent Select Committee on Intelligence.

When the call was answered somewhere near Langley, Virginia, and transferred to the intended party, she simply said, "It's time."

The murders, the countless interviews of young Maria, the miles of paperwork, and the subsequent phone call to Virginia had all taken place three weeks earlier. In the meantime, an outstanding US Army Ranger, with a native grasp of the Spanish language, had recently returned from Afghanistan. There were inquiries, files pulled, calls made, and it was already decided—Sergeant Joseph Chandler just might be the man.

CHAPTER 9

CIA 201

Mexico

Joe's flight from Bagram Air Force to Andrews in Washington DC landed at 7:50 AM. Fortunately, he had gotten a few hours of sleep after the layover in Germany. His commanding officer at Ft. Benning had sent him orders to report to the George Bush Center for Intelligence in Langley, Virginia. A car had been sent for him and the Marine driver, once through the gated checkpoint, had dropped him in front of a familiar office building. Again, an MP escorted him down a long hall, an elevator ride up two floors, and through a set of double doors. In minutes, Colonel Pike's smiling face appeared and welcomed Joe home.

"We're very proud of you, Sergeant Chandler, and there are some people waiting to meet you. Please follow me."

Joe was looking forward to rejoining the 75th Rangers at Fort Bennington and, quite honestly, he'd seen this movie before and he was a bit concerned.

When he and Pike entered the large office, a man in a suit, without introducing himself, said, "I took a look at your linguist records. Arabic and Spanish—where did a gringo get such a command of the Spanish language?"

"Well, sir, there is a family by the name of Palmero who lived with us since I was a child. His English was marginal at best, and hers was almost nonexistent. We used to sing a lot, sir."

The man considered that for a moment then said, "Yes, we Mexicans do like to sing. Please, have a seat. I also see by this report from Afghanistan you know how to get things done."

"I had a great team, sir, and we caught a few breaks."

The man looked down at the file and then back at Joe.

"It looks to me, Sergeant Chandler, like you created most of your own breaks. Regardless, nice job and now there are some things we need you to consider. If you agree to help us, Sergeant, as usual, they'll be a bit of paperwork. I'll leave you gentlemen to it."

The man rose and without acknowledging anyone else, walked out of the office. Joe looked at Colonel Pike who had his arms crossed and a grin on his face.

"Excuse me, sir, but I get the feeling you are about to reassign me again."

"Sergeant, I can't tell you a great deal until you are formally read into the mission. However, I promise that you will have the chance to rejoin the 75th or request another assignment if you refuse this mission and no one will think the less of you. Let's get you downstairs and some formalities out of the way and everything will be explained in detail."

Outside the office, two Military Policemen confirmed his ID and escorted him down a long hallway, a flight of stairs, and through multiple security doors. IDs were checked and rechecked. There were searches and inspections of orders, but finally they arrived at an empty office where he was instructed to have a seat and wait. His escorts stood outside the door until they were dismissed by a commanding female voice.

"That will be all, gentlemen. Thank you very much."

A beautiful woman of Hispanic descent walked in reading a file, sat down, and did not look up for quite some time. Still reading, she smiled and shook her head.

"Well corporal, if only you boys would live up to your reputation, we'd get along just fine, but you guys rarely do."

"Actually it's Sergeant, ma'am. I'm not a corporal."

When she did look up right into those ridiculously green eyes, she lost her train of thought and got a bit flustered. Trying to regain her composure, she looked back at the file.

"What I was going to say Corp—uh, Sergeant," as she looked at the file again; "was" then she did it again. Her face flushed and she completely lost her thoughts.

"I apologize, ma'am; I hope I didn't offend you."

"Uhhh, no, ah... no, not at all. It's that I was expecting another knuckle dragger from Special Forces and well, you... uhhh... oh, never mind!"

Finally regaining her composure, she continued reading.

"So, you are from the 75th and you are a linguist, and I do see here you are a sergeant—I apologize. Your test scores are remarkable. Hmm, let's see: you have a degree in political science with a minor in Middle Eastern studies—is that correct, Sergeant?"

"Yes, ma'am, that is correct."

"Quite frankly, I'm surprised you didn't take another career path and be somewhere other than here."

"I'm sure that's what my parents are thinking, and with all due respect, ma'am, I'm not exactly sure what I *am* doing here, but I assume either you or someone will explain."

Quietly, yet a bit too audibly, she mumbled something about modeling, but finally cleared her throat and formally introduced herself.

"First of all, my name is Ms. Mendez and I'm going to have you sign a few disclosures stating that you will be shot if you repeat anything you read or hear in this meeting or any such meetings going forward. Is that clear?"

She removed a sizeable stack of papers from her folder and asked Joe to read them carefully. Assuming he would do as all the others, she instructed him accordingly.

"Take your time and make sure you know what you're signing. Or if not, please initial each page at the bottom then sign and date the last page."

Ms. Mendez was surprised and somewhat disappointed as Joe began reading page one. She glanced at her watch, but much quicker than she expected, he seemed to actually read and comprehend each page. He asked a few pertinent questions and even pointed out a misspelled word on page thirty-eight.

"All right, I believe I got it." After signing the last page, he laid down his pen. Ms. Mendez looked at him for a moment then pushed a button on the phone. Immediately, another woman—this one a very attractive Navy lieutenant—walked in, looked at the file, confirming each initial and the signature before taking it with her. When she turned to walk out, Joe was standing at attention.

"At ease, soldier. If you keep doing that in this building, you're going to get a cramp. There's enough brass around here to outfit several orchestras. Unless a colonel, a general, or the president walks in, feel free to keep your seat."

Then the lieutenant glanced at his butt, looked at Ms. Mendez, raised her eyebrows, smiled, and left the room. Ms. Mendez did not like the lieutenant, nor did she like the insinuation the lieutenant made with her eyes.

"Please sit down, Sergeant."

Ms. Mendez explained to Joe that he was going to be "read-in," as the saying goes, to some extremely sensitive and top-secret information.

Although it sounded somewhat condescending, she said, "Regardless of the pretty lieutenant's laissez-faire demeanor, she is an attorney and has the necessary credentials to brief you."

It was quiet obvious that it pained Ms. Mendez terribly to lend any credence whatsoever to the pretty lieutenant. Joe didn't miss much, including how fit Ms. Mendez was, and that she carried herself like a woman not to be messed with. He knew it was pouring gas on a raging fire but he couldn't help himself.

"Yeah, she is rather pretty, isn't she?"

Ms. Mendez's eyes narrowed, her lips seemed to stiffen, and with obvious reluctance picked up the phone, pressed the same button, and after a few seconds said, "We're ready."

Immediately the cute Navy lieutenant walked back in and asked Joe to follow her. Several turns and one large set of double doors later, they entered a secure conference room where she pointed toward a chair and asked him to have a seat. She opened another file and, looking a bit more serious, told him to pay attention. Joe nodded and she began unfolding a condensed version of two years of surveillance, intelligence, and research on an operation she referred to as *Widow Maker.* She pulled five pictures, all of death and destruction, from the file. There were bodies, bombed out buildings, and previous gangsters who were hanging from a bridge.

"These unfortunate souls used to work for our target." She pulled out the last two pictures. The first was a Mexican man, twenty-nine years of age. He was wearing dark sunglasses and a natural silk jacket.

"Recognize him?"

"Sure, I just saved his life in Afghanistan."

"We think he works for a man who recently ordered this." She shoved the last picture across the table. It showed the bodies of sixteen dead teenage girls from Guatemala.

"I think this was the final straw. Are there any questions?"

Joe indicated there was none.

"All right, then: follow me and I'll show you to the exit. There is a car waiting to take you to a nice hotel." She handed him a government credit card and a prepaid cell phone.

"If I were you, Sergeant Chandler, I would order room service and think about all this. That will be all for today. Keep your mouth shut and eyes open, okay?"

She walked him to the door and stood there, smiling mischievously. "If there's anything left when these guys are done with you, give me a call and I'll buy you a drink."

She eyed him from top to bottom, grabbed his arm and wrote a name and cell number on his wrist, then turned to walk away. "So be careful, Chandler; it would be such a waste."

While Joe was used to women flirting, passing him notes, and writing their phone numbers on his arm, that was then and this was now. He'd been in the Army for over three years and the idea of a Navy lieutenant making a pass at him, especially while both were in uniform, made him very uncomfortable. Joe, drawing on all the composure he could muster, looked at his shoes and nodded. Besides, what he was really thinking about was her statement: *"If there's anything left when these guys are through with you."*

Two days passed when Joe's burner phone rang. It woke him out of a deep sleep. He had taken the lieutenant's advice and ordered room service, a lot, and watched TV and slept... a lot. He opened his eyes, saw sunlight, and grabbed the phone. "Be downstairs in fifteen minutes; a car will be waiting."

Joe stepped out the front door of the hotel and walked toward a female airman in her dress blues standing next to an ugly vehicle that could be nothing but government-issued. They made the short drive to Langley, parked, and she asked Joe to follow her. It was the same building as before, only the third floor.

"If you'll have a seat, Sergeant, someone will be along for you shortly."

After what seemed like an eternity, an Air Force sergeant appeared and asked Joe to follow him. The young man, short and a bit plump, wore his dress blues but looked more like a character from a Disney sitcom. His badge identified him as intel but still, thought Joe, *This guy must be the poster boy for armed services nerd.*

The young man led Joe through some doors requiring a scan from a card hanging from a lanyard he wore around his neck. Next, they arrived at a metal detector where Joe surrendered his cell phone and what felt like his future. Continuing on, Joe finally arrived at the desk of a familiar face. The nameplate on the glass door surprised him—*GABRIELA MENDEZ, ASSISTANT DIRECTOR, LATIN AMERICAN AFFAIRS.*

"Hello again, Sergeant. I'm Gabriela Mendez. If you remember, we met two days ago."

How could I forget, thought Joe. "Yes, I recall some confusion about my rank. It's nice to see you again, Ms. Mendez."

"Sergeant, if you have any question, any reservations, now is the time."

Truth was he wasn't sure what he thought, and until he knew exactly what this was all about, he decided to withhold his reservations and said nothing.

She looked at Joe, trying to read him, but he didn't concede much in his body language.

"Very well then... if you are sure." Yet again, she pushed another button. "Whenever the director is ready? Yes, sir, we're on our way."

Joe wondered exactly how many buttons did Ms. Mendez push. She stood, exited her office with Joe in tow, and walked past an Army major who didn't acknowledge them. Joe on the other hand glanced nervously out the corner of his eye as he still wasn't comfortable walking past an officer without acknowledging them. Gabby entered without knocking and took a seat, leaving Joe as the only one standing. Joe did, however, see a familiar face sitting behind the large, intricately engraved mahogany desk. When that man stood, so did the others in the room. He extended his hand.

"Good to see you again, Sergeant. My name is Raphael Valenzuela. Most of these impolite, ill-bread bastards call me Ralph. You may call me Director or sir. Have a seat."

Joe sat in the only empty chair next to Gabby as the other three in the room finished a private conversation.

"Breathe," whispered Gabby. "You'll get used to it and, besides, you're the guest of honor."

Finally, everyone's eyes focused on a man unfamiliar to Joe; the man dimmed the lights and began the slide presentation. A picture of a rather chubby Latino man appeared and was identified as Juan Delmar Espinoza. Joe figured him as the bad guy since they used all three of his names, which was soon confirmed by Director Valenzuela.

"Sergeant, this is a bad son of a bitch. I want you to find him and, if the opportunity arises, kill him."

The man doing the slide show continued with the details, including Espinoza's family, security details, and known associates.

"He moves around quite a bit, but currently he is in Costa Rica posing as a rich Mexican industrialist on vacation with his wife and two daughters. He's damn sure rich, but his wealth does not come from manufacturing anything but drugs, death, and misery."

The director wrapped up the meeting. "Chandler, you got into the middle of this thing in Afghanistan and we thought you might wish to finish it. We're fairly certain the man you snagged in the Arghandab River Valley works for this jackass and we'd be honored if you would see this through.

"Your partner is well informed on the logistics of the operation. You'll be brought up to speed in the next few days. You need to head down to Tucson and meet Sherriff Monroe Culpepper. He's a good man and you'll need to pay attention. From there, you'll fly to Cozumel, Mexico, where you'll meet the rest of your team. As soon as we can confirm, you will receive an updated report on the whereabouts of Mr. Espinoza. Any questions?"

"Yes, sir: you mentioned a partner and I was wondering how soon I would meet him?"

Everyone in the room chuckled and glanced at Gabby. "You already have, Sergeant, and he's a she."

Joe felt his cheeks redden when the director laughed and said, "It's a changing world, Sergeant, that's for damn sure, but you couldn't be in more capable hands. Pay attention and she just might bring your ass back alive."

The director rose, stuck out his hand, which Joe shook, and he was whisked away by the ever-surprising Ms. Gabriela Mendez.

Without saying a word, Joe followed her toward an exit. Halfway down the hall, she stopped and leaned against a wall. "We'll be traveling quite a bit together, mostly out of country, so obviously 'Sergeant' won't work. From here on out you call me Gabby and unless there is another name you prefer, I plan to call you Joe—is that okay?"

Joe was quiet for a moment. "So, am I exclusively contracted to the CIA? I mean, I guess it doesn't matter but I just need to get things right in my head."

Gabby looked at him hesitantly and then, with a note of compassion, said, "Look, Sergeant, we both work for the United States of America and we both are sworn to defend her. The titles on the letterheads won't mean much where we're going, so get your head straight and don't worry, I'm a lot more comfortable in the field than behind a desk. Someone will meet you out front at 6:00 AM, so grab your gear and you'll be shown to your temporary quarters here at the campus. Get some sleep because tomorrow you start training. Good day, Sergeant."

"That's fine, ma'am, but you should start calling me Joe."

"I'll call you Joe, but if you call me 'ma'am' one more time, I swear…."

Walking away, Gabby smiled and thought, *Okay, Joe, you just might be the man.*

CHAPTER 10

The Mayor's Party

As they made their way down the mile-long driveway lined with beautiful, maple, raywood ash, and giant fir trees, Mel's eyes widened like a child seeing Disneyland for the first time. The grounds, resembling more of a professional golf course than yard, were afire with twinkling lights that swept down to the banks of the Umpqua River. As they pulled around the circular drive, a young man in a tux offered valet parking.

"I checked the mileage," said Joe as he handed the lad the keys to his corvette.

"My goodness, I had no idea. Who is this guy, an oil baron?"

"He's very wealthy," said Joe, "but it's not from oil. His father was the largest private owner of timberland in the Western United States. He's rich but he's a good man, and he's been a very good friend to me."

They were escorted to the festivities in the backyard where a chamber orchestra was playing and friends were mingling. There were more than one hundred of Donovan County's richest—and most generous—gathered to open their checkbook for yet another of the mayor's fundraisers. Tonight's occasion would benefit a college fund for the children of Oregon policemen and military veterans killed in the line of duty. It was going to be an expensive evening for all the guests, but they were generous and the dozen cases of wine from local vineyards were certain to grease the skids.

Suddenly there was a shrill, which almost stopped the music. Fortunately, everyone was used to Jillian Abercrombe's vivacious demeanor.

"Joe, darling, I thought you would never get here. How absolutely boring the evening would have been if you stood me up."

After a kiss on his cheek, Jillian looked at Mel, "My goodness, Joe, who is this beautiful girl?"

"Jillian, may I present Michele Randle. Mel, this is Jillian Abercrombe, our host and wife of Steelhead's illustrious mayor."

"Illustrious? Ha! More like scandalous. He is beginning to ignore me, Joe, and I will not have it. Since this whole nonsense with Bill Crivelli, he is a mess. You will talk to him, won't you, Joe? He adores you. Oh, for heaven sakes, where are my manners! Ms. Randle, do forgive me."

"Oh, please, call me Mel. I would be honored and feel much more comfortable if you do."

"Thank you, Mel—only if you call me Jillian. As I was saying, Joe is more like family, and he seems to be one of the few my husband listens to. Come along, dear, let's show you off and dash the hopes of half the women here."

Mel glanced at Joe, crossed her eyes and puffed out her cheeks like a blowfish, which made him smile, then grabbed his arm and followed Jillian into battle. There were lots of introductions, a few disheartened stares from women, but the men, who had been drinking for quiet-some-time, paid close attention to the girl on Joe's arm. Mel was wearing a black pantsuit with a sequin jacket and a stunning silver and turquoise necklace adorned her long, sleek neck. No doubt about it, every eye at the party was on Mel Randle. Someone grabbed Joe and started talking politics and, unfortunately, Mel was left with Leonard Tettleman.

"You will save me a dance won't you, darling?"

Leonard was wider than he was tall and got a sudden pinch from his wife who excused the both of them. Mel felt someone grab her hand and to her great relief, turned to see Lizzie.

"Well, you ran the gauntlet, my dear, and I must say you did so with great poise. I was afraid poor Leonard was about to embarrass himself worse than he did. He really is a doll until his fourth glass of wine. Come join us. We're sitting with the Abecrombes, and Drummer can't wait to be seen with you. We'll leave Joe to the wolves for a while. Once he figures out you've disappeared, he'll be along."

Drummer rose and gave Mel a warm hug and peck on the cheek, and then he and Lizzie doted over her as though she had been in their lives for years. Joe escaped the political bickering without choosing sides and took a seat. Finally free of his social duties, the mayor joined his table. Before Joe could do the introductions, the mayor walked over and stood behind Mel.

"Young lady, I have been watching you all evening and I must say you have graced us and are the belle of the ball. Please accept my sincere apologies for being late."

At that, Joe said, "Mel, this much older man flirting with you is Mayor Hobie Abercrombe. Hobie, may I present Ms. Michele Randle."

Hobie leaned in and quietly insisted they both stick around once the festivities were done.

Many danced, some drank too much, but in the end it was a huge success for the benefactors of the generous donations. Finally, after the last lingering guests were escorted to their cars, Jillian gave a long sigh and said, "My God, I love those people but I'm so glad to see their taillights I could just scream 'Yahoo!'"

Joe shook his head, Mel smiled, and Drummer and Lizzie yelled, "Yahoo!"

Hobie, who had disappeared, hollered from the back door and waved everyone inside. Belts were loosened, shoes were removed, and decaf coffee was served by an older gentleman named Carlyle.

"If there is nothing more, Mr. Abercrombe, I will retire."

"Goodnight, Carlyle!" yelled everyone but Mel.

The distinguished gentleman with a thick British accent turned and quietly disappeared.

"I've been trying to get him to call me Hobie for over twenty years, but I've given up. We met him in England about twenty-five years ago. He and his wife owned a small but exquisite bed and breakfast where Jillian and I had stayed. Upon our return, we were heartbroken to learn he had lost his wife to cancer the previous summer. When we discovered he didn't have the heart to continue without her, we invited him to come and visit us. He said, 'Only if I can make myself useful.' Fortunately he did come, and thank God he's never left."

"I never tire of that story, Hobie," said Lizzie. "And I can't imagine this place without Carlyle."

"Oh, Lord, me either," said Jillian. "Hobie would be a grumpy ole butt if he depended on me to wait on him; I swear he'd rid the place of me before he'd let go of Carlyle."

"Not true, my dear, I'd be equally distraught to lose either of you."

They all enjoyed a good laugh.

"Now," said Hobie, "let's get down to business. Ms. Randle, it is my understanding you are in big demand back down there in the smog and that bumper-to-bumper pressure cooker called California. Certainly you understand we weren't created to live like that. It darkens your soul and I cannot sit idly by and let that happen to you."

Mel's mouth was open as she looked contemptuously at Joe, whose eyes were wider than usual. Joe shook his head, knowing what she must be thinking, so they both looked back at Hobie.

"Look here, Mel. Joe doesn't know a thing about this, but I believe when opportunity knocks, you're an idiot if you don't try and pull it through the door."

"Mel," said Drummer rather apprehensively. "I'm afraid I'm guilty of collusion as well. I went to San Francisco to meet with a group of wine distributors and while I was there, Hobie asked if I'd nose around a little."

"Me? It was as much your idea as mine! Well, it's like this, Mel," continued Hobie. "Archie Anderson is a very dear friend of mine and has been the DA in Steelhead for nineteen years. He was instrumental in getting me to run for mayor and has had my back through some nasty lies and attacks. One of those sorry bastards, forgive my French, is a man named Bill Crivelli. He was a hatchet man for Dr. John Grossman, that charlatan who was impeached as an Oregon congressman."

"Not before he and his buddies misplaced three hundred million dollars and left town," added Drummer.

"It's a long story, Mel," said Hobie, "but Archie has taken a great deal of direct fire. Crivelli has some powerful friends and they really went after him. Sexual harassment, bribes, discrimination, you name it and these ruthless dogs unleashed it all on poor Archie. Because of the investigation, his license is suspended and the truth is I'm not sure he'll ever be the same. Anyway, it's not a flattering proposal, Ms. Randle, but we would like to offer you the position as assistant district attorney. Of course, it won't pay near as much as you could make down in California, but the truth is we could really use your help right now."

There was a very long, awkward silence and Mel broke it even more awkwardly.

"Look, everybody. First, let me say how flattered I am ... I think. However, with all due respect, you must be out of your minds. I *just* graduated from law school. I have not had one single job as an attorney, much less any experience as a DA. In fact, that's so far off my radar; I'm not sure what they do except prosecute criminals who show up in court with much better paid counsel. Secondly, I'm not even licensed to practice law in Oregon, yet you want me to walk into the middle of some age-old vendetta. This Crivelli has already undermined an experienced prosecutor, one who's forgotten more about the criminal justice system of Oregon than I'll ever know. Did I forget anything?"

"No, that pretty well covered it," said Hobie. "However, in the interim, I would like your help with some contract issues that my company has with the Department of the Interior. It pays well and it will give you a chance to learn the lay of the land while you're getting your license to practice law in Oregon. An expense, by the way, we are happy to absorb."

"Oh, my God!" Mel screamed. Well, not really screamed, but there was definitely some emotion in her voice. "Again, with all due respect, you're crazy, certifiably crazy for even proposing this to me. Are you sure you're not part of this insane scheme?" she said, glaring at Joe.

"Absolutely not. Honestly, Mel, I'm as blindsided here as you, and if you want to leave I'm ready when you are."

Joe looked at both his father and Hobie as though he would later kill them in their sleep.

"Hang on a second," said Drummer. "Both of you just hang on for one dad-gum second. First of all, Mel, Louie Trudeau is a very good friend of mine."

"Wait!" said Mel. "Dr. Louis Trudeau, my criminal law professor, not to mention probably the most influential professor at Stanford Law—that Louie Trudeau?"

"Yes, Mel, *that* Louie Trudeau. I called him and asked if we could have coffee. Back in the day, Louie was *da man* on a bass guitar. I bounced this crazy idea off him and he laughed. He said you were one of the hardest-working and most promising students he'd had in a decade. He laughed again and said I was definitely dreaming if I had any illusion of you staying in—and I quote—'Podunk Oregon.' He said you were a hot commodity and would be recruited by some corporate law firm, and probably a partner in five years. Then do you know what else he said? He said it's really too bad, because if ever he'd seen a naturally gifted prosecutor, it was you. I realize Hobie and I have overstepped our boundaries, and we know it. It's just that you were here and not there, and, well, it was a long shot, Mel. We didn't mean to insult you, and if we did, please forgive us."

Mel blew out a long breath then looked at Drummer. "Dr. Trudeau played the bass?"

"Oh, darling, he could make a bass guitar talk and sing in two languages. As I remember, he dropped out of Berkley right before he graduated and joined a group called Cherry something or another. Unfortunately they were a one-hit wonder and faded away, but every band in the country that needed a bass player wanted to hire Louie. Anyway, he toured for a year, made a name for himself in the studios, and then disappeared. Next thing I know I'm reading about this high-profile prosecutor in LA who was locking up some very dangerous people. Rumor had it the Hells Angels and the Mafia were arguing over who was going to kill him. Subsequently, he disappeared for several years and the next thing I know I see he's a law professor at Stanford."

"And he actually said I was a naturally-gifted prosecutor?"

"Yes, Mel, that's exactly what he said."

"Well, I stand by my earlier statement."

"You mean that we're all certifiably insane?"

"No, that I am flattered and I mean it. Thank you all; I needed the vote of confidence more than you can imagine, and I have to admit I am having second thoughts about the direction of my career. Regardless, to take on the jobs as assistant DA and unlicensed counsel to sue the federal government, I mean ... holy cow! You folks sure know how to entertain the new girl in town."

"Well, at least sleep on it," suggested Hobie. "The offer stands and I'm sure we can negotiate a salary commensurate with your current income."

Mel smiled as she and Joe stood, said goodnight to everyone, and headed for the car.

Back inside, the mood was hopeful.

"You should both be ashamed," said Lizzie.

"I agree," said Jillian. "But wouldn't it be something if these two conniving boys of ours pulled it off?"

"Delightful. Absolutely delightful," said Lizzie. "And I'm pretty sure Joe wouldn't mind a bit."

After saying goodnight, the Chandlers also took their leave and enjoyed the late night ride home. As usual, they had the top down and some seventies rock blaring from the stereo of the convertible BMW.

CHAPTER 11

George Bush Center for Intelligence

Langley, Virginia

Joe figured the Ranger Indoctrination Program, along with his experience, had prepared him for anything he'd face in the field, so the idea of additional training seemed redundant. Stopping at an in-house kiosk, Gabby ordered two black coffees and sat down at a small table.

"Most CIA field operatives spend two years training for their careers and missions. Several people above my pay grade decided this might be more of a military-style op, so here you are, Joe. Today you are going to report to, recently retired, Chief Petty Officer Mac Dumont. After sixteen years and hundreds of missions as a Navy SEAL, Mac finished his twenty as a trainer at BUD/S out in Coronado. He's a little scary but he teaches our field and clandestine officers some invaluable stuff. He's put together a program custom-designed for situations like this. Since it's such a short course, he calls it WOS-E. It's an acronym for weapons, observation, survival, and evasion. The standard program is an intense three-month training exercise and you are going to get it in five days, so pay attention."

"No problem, Gabby. I survived seven hours of shopping on Black Friday with my mom. I did recon for lingerie, evaded hundreds of hostile shoppers, and had to disarm an angry housewife who was about to take a swing at my mom with a toilet brush. This will be a piece of cake."

Gabby looked unamused by the humor as she furrowed her brow and squinted her eyes. "This might be a bit different, Joe. Please pay attention: I do not want you embarrassing me, understood? Unless you crap out sooner, we'll have your review from Mac by Saturday morning, and if it goes well, we'll get our orders."

Their first stop at 6:00 AM was the Office of Asian Pacific, Latin American, and African Analysis. At 6:45, after looking at satellite photos, they walked across a parking lot and hopped in the back of what looked like a cross between a bus and golf cart. By 7:00 AM, they were at the weapons center where Mac was waiting outside. Gabby had mentioned a retired Navy chief, so Joe was not expecting the lean, fit man who shook his hand.

"Welcome aboard, Sergeant. You got nice reviews in your file but I'm not expecting much. If Ms. Mendez will excuse us, we'll go see if it's all BS."

At that, the two men walked away in the direction of automatic gunfire.

At 08:00 AM on Saturday morning, Joe and Gabby were sitting in an office with Lt. Col. Pike who, after reading Joe's results, looked up and smiled.

"All right, you two are a GO. Chandler, Mac says you—and I quote—'*are a smart, tough son of a bitch who was sneaky enough to shake all of my best observers.*' He said you learned your weapons with exceptional speed," and once again, he quoted Mac, "*In spite of him being Army, I'd go into battle with this soldier.*"

Joe was looking down at the file but Gabby was beaming like a proud parent at a teacher's conference.

Lt. Col Pike continued, "I will be your intelligence liaison throughout the entire op. You will receive as much good information as I can safely get you, and it will be my job to extract you once your mission is complete. Sherriff Monroe Culpepper, down in Tucson, is expecting you both. It looks like we've confirmed that your man, Espinoza, was responsible for the death of those sixteen young girls in San Miguel. They were all from Guatemala and the one survivor, a Maria Perez, is currently in the custody of Pima County authorities. It also looks like the sheriff may have arrested the shooter. Apparently, he's an illegal with a prior arrest and has been deported twice. I want you to talk to them both. From Tucson, you will fly to Cozumel where our people are waiting to meet you. You'll assume your new identities immediately. You will be traveling as husband and wife on your way to one of those fashionable eco tours in Costa Rica. If there are no other questions, you've earned a thirty-six-hour pass. Your flight to Tucson leaves Sunday at 1630 hours. Now go practice being married. Ah, dang it, forget I said that. Go to dinner, do anything but get out of my office before I say something else stupid. Good luck and Godspeed."

They thanked the colonel and got down the hall at least twenty yards before they both burst into laughter.

"He's right," said Gabby. "We should let the Agency buy us a nice dinner and at least one bottle of good wine, don't you think, Joe?"

"Sure, I guess that would be all right."

"Wow, don't sound so enthusiastic. It was simply a casual suggestion, but please don't feel obligated."

"No, it's not that I don't want to do it. Really, it sounds fun but it's just that, well, I don't know."

"Oh, great. Well, now's the time Joe, but if you tell me you're gay, I'm going to be very professional about it but I will be a little disappointed."

"What! No, it's nothing like that. It's just I've had all this training for the last three years and, well, I don't really know anything about being married. And the truth is I don't want to do something stupid and blow our mission."

"Joseph Chandler, you are a piece of work. I'll pick you up at six and you better look nice because I'm wearing a dress."

Joe was still standing there watching her walk away. He smiled and thought to himself, *So, she would be disappointed—good to know.*

Dinner was at Giuseppe's Ristorante, a nice atmosphere with white tablecloths and candles. The food was excellent, as was the bottle of Oregon wine.

"Segundo Vida Vineyards," said Gabby, reading the label. "Nice call. I don't think I've ever drank Tempranillo. This is very good. Have you had it before?"

"Yeah, once or twice."

"Oh, that's right, you're from Oregon. You should find this place and buy a case."

"Good idea," said Joe.

CHAPTER 12

TUCSON, ARIZONA

Chasing the sun and picking up three hours on the flight west, Joe and Gabby arrived in Tucson before eight o'clock in the evening. Joe had an amazing sixth sense and his sharp eyes missed very little, but Gabby was the experienced field agent and, as planned, she would handle the questions and interrogations.

Back at the Agency, because he asked, Lt. Col. Pike had told Joe a little about Gabby. She was from a solid diplomatic family in upstate New York and a Yale graduate with a degree in international relations. She made the Olympic biathlon team but, during a family ski trip to Canada, Gabby dislocated her shoulder. Regardless, because she lied about the severity of her pain, she still made the team. She was out-shooting everyone but, eventually, the team doctor figured out the seriousness of her injury. Needless to say, she was extremely disappointed. The FBI noticed her first and approached her about a career. However, when Raphael Valenzuela got wind of her shooting skills and her GPA from Yale, the Bureau never had a chance.

On Monday morning, Joe and Gabby were greeted by Sherriff Monroe Culpepper.

"I'm not exactly sure who in the Sam Hill you two are, and I'm pretty sure I don't want to know, but I've got orders from Ralph to cooperate and that's good enough for me. That jackass and I go back a long way and I think a lot of him. Get in the car and we'll grab us a Starbucks on the way to Social Services. It pains me terribly to pay $4.00 for a damn cup of coffee, so I'll let Ralph pick up the bill. Is that a problem?"

"Absolutely not," said Gabby. "As a matter of fact, maybe we can buy lunch once we've had a chance to visit with your two guests."

"Okay, sounds good to me. Ralph has a hell of a lot more money in his budget than these greedy county commissioners give me. However, you may want to take your time with this young girl, Maria Perez. I'm sure this whole ordeal shook her; hell, it ought too, but I think she's street-smart and I get the feeling she's anxious to bury the man responsible for all this. Two of the younger girls were from her little community in Guatemala. Apparently she's in no hurry to get back to her grandmother, so she might be of some help. We haven't got much out of her, but Ralph said to wait on you."

Gabby told the boys to wait outside and she spent the next hour and a half sitting next to Maria on a big sofa. When he first peeked through the glass door, Gabby was doing all the talking. Later when Joe peeked again, Maria was waving her arms around and talking up a storm. Finally, Gabby walked out.

"I'm hungry. Where can we get some good buttermilk pancakes?"

Joe and Monroe looked at each other and shrugged.

"Get in. We'll go to Bobos, but nobody breathes a word of this to my wife."

Halfway through a large stack, Gabby looked up from her plate. "What?"

"I've just never seen a woman attack pancakes like a South Georgia trucker. And besides," said Monroe, "I'd sure like to know what that little girl said."

Gabby finished off her last pancake, washed it down with the remainder of her milk. "Sherriff, I could tell you but I'd have to kill you."

Monroe's eyes squinted as he looked over at Joe. "She's kidding, right?"

Joe shrugged his shoulders, and they both turned and looked at Gabby.

"Yeah, just kidding, Sheriff. You were right, though: the girl is not stupid, and dropping and playing dead—that was more instinct than luck. Our little Maria has been arrested for pickpocketing tourists in Ixcán, and supported her grandma by running backpacks between sellers and buyers."

"Drugs?" asked Monroe.

"She thinks so; but she never asked, and no one mentioned it. However, she did see a man killed once during a drop. She said she hid and watched a man pull a pistol and shoot the other man between the eyes. She said it was the same man who killed the girls."

"Why in heaven's name did Maria get in that truck?" asked Joe. "Especially if she knew what this creep was capable of? She sounds like a crafty veteran of the streets, so I'm surprised they ever caught her."

"Yup, I asked her the same thing," said Gabby. "She was watching when the same man snatched two small girls in an alley as they were playing with an old tire. He asked them to look at something in the back of his truck, then pushed them in and closed the door. Our little Maria jumped on the bumper and held on for dear life. She tried to open the latch but couldn't. The truck pulled into a warehouse before she could jump off. They held them in a large room with a woman who beat them if they yelled or cried. Maria said she heard the driver tell someone on the phone that he would make the drop and bring back someone named Charley. She couldn't hear well but it sounded like he was bringing back two men. That's when they were loaded into a semitrailer without food or water. She said every two days someone opened the little door and threw in a sack of tacos and one gallon of water. She said there was no place to pee. She thinks they traveled from the region of Ixcán to what she believes was Chihuahua, Mexico. She heard men yelling about money and fighting about who was going to take the girls once they got into the United States. Then a man from Chihuahua opened the door and started screaming about how ugly and skinny the girls were. He pulled two little ones out and stripped them and then he yelled some more. He pulled the girls back into the trailer by their hair. That's when Maria said she heard the man called Tino, the one driving the truck, say that Señor Espinoza would kill the other men if he didn't get his money and the two 'Mikes.' Maria said it was confusing, but she understood they were being traded for two men named Charley and Mike. She said they slammed the doors shut and she was very afraid they would die. I asked her why and she said, '*Because we all saw the men's faces.*' No, sir: this girl is not stupid."

"It wasn't *Charleys and Mikes,*" said Joe. "It was motorcycles, two Harley bikes. He was trading the girls for money and two Harley Davidson bikes."

"Yes, siree," said the sheriff. "You're probably right, Joe. We arrested the driver of the truck at a Harley Davidson dealer."

"What great value our Señor Espinoza puts on the lives of young girls," said Gabby. "Sheriff, let's go talk to the driver. Maybe I'll take him a taco and a bottle of water."

Sheriff Culpepper nodded and led the way to the exit.

As they were driving toward the correction facility, Joe leaned in from the backseat. "Gabby, are you okay or do you always eat like a professional wrestler?"

Gabby turned with a serious stare. "Only when I'm really pissed, Joe; it's what I do—I eat buttermilk pancakes. It calms me down so I can think past the anger—anything else?"

"Nope, I'm good."

For the time being, Tino Alvarez was isolated at the Pima County Adult Detention Center, a minimum-security facility in Tucson, which made every law enforcement entity and government agency involved very nervous. In the meantime, the local sheriff's department, the FBI, the DEA, and the Department of Homeland Security were fighting to see who would eventually take custody and begin prosecution. However, standing in everyone's way was Danny Mora, attorney-at-law. Mr. Mora was not only a smart litigator, he was also chairman of the Cesar Chavez Foundation and currently serving on the board of directors for the National Council of La Raza, as well as the Mexican American Legal Defense. And, as expected, because Mr. Mora was involved, things slowed down.

A call was made to Langley and another call was made to Homeland Security and finally, at 4:59 PM, one to Mr. Mora. When he learned his client was about to be interviewed without his presence, he threatened to sue the federal government. After learning a terrorist charge was now on the table and his client would be exempt from his rights to legal counsel, Danny Mora swore loudly, said they wouldn't get away with it, and slammed down the phone. Of course he was right to be upset, but the bluff made by a first-year clerk at the CIA gave Gabby and Joe the hour they needed. In the meantime, Mr. Mora scrambled furiously to find a judge who would stay the questionable order. That was the primary reason they make the call at five o'clock: like everyone else, federal judges are much harder to find after office hours.

The three entered the facility together, and having the sheriff along did not hurt a thing. However, once inside and the suspect was safely cuffed and secured, the sheriff was excused.

"Do you want me to wait as well?" asked Joe.

"No, not this time. Tino's culture and machismo prohibits him from giving me any respect. I want his attention quickly, and I think it will help if you are in the room. Follow my lead and if you see an opening, follow your instincts. Besides, he's going to get nervous when his attorney doesn't show up. Let's go see if we can scare him into making a deal."

Tino Alvarez tried to show a little attitude when Joe and Gabby walked in, but you could tell his heart just wasn't in it. He looked at the two of them.

"I'm not saying *mierda, nada*... until my attorney gets here."

"Oh," said Gabby. "You must be talking about Mr. Mora and I don't think he's your attorney anymore. And besides, he's not coming, so you can stop staring at the door."

"Why he no come? Why he no my lawyer no more?"

"Well, Tino, it's like this: since we're holding you as a terrorist, I'm not sure but I don't think an attorney will help you. And I think when Mr. Mora learned that there were two eyewitnesses who saw you kill those little girls, I'm almost certain he didn't have the stomach to see you hang."

"Nobody saw me shoot *esas niñas. Nadie!*"

"If you don't speak English, Tino, if you don't understand, I will bring in an interpreter, *entender?*

"I understand very good, señorita, *no problemo.* Nobody saw me shoot nobody, no little girls, nobody. You understand, and what you mean terrorist? I no terrorist and nobody hangs no nobody no more. No in America."

Mel looked at Joe who took a deep breath and leaned in close to Tino.

"Okay, amigo. We came to try to save you from being hanged as a terrorist. That's what they do now, Tino. I think the presidente—you know, the one who promises to build the wall—he says he'll hang terrorist. And if your lawyer does come back, which I doubt, and says you're not going to hang, he probably voted for the lady to be presidente, amigo, and she lost.

Tino was obviously disturbed by the idea of being hanged, and Joe had his undivided attention. "It's like this, Tino: you kidnapped those girls in Guatemala. We have an eyewitness who is ready to testify. Next, you drove those girls to Chihuahua, Mexico, where you argued with two men about the money and the motorcycles. In fact, you told them your boss, Juan Delmar Espinoza, would kill them if their people in the US didn't give you the money and the two Harleys. Are you listening, Tino?"

When Juan Espinoza's name was mentioned, Tino had simply smiled; not the response Joe was expecting, so Joe reached out and slapped him across his face.

"You brought those girls to Arizona, Tino, and something happened. The deal went south, *mal tartan*, and when you told your boss, Señor Espinoza, the girls had seen you, he told you to kill them. We know all about it, Tino. The Harley dealer has already identified you. When he asked too many questions about registering the bikes, you got scared, Tino—you got scared and you threatened him. That was stupid, amigo. You never threaten a Harley Davidson dealer. When he saw you thinking about pulling your gun, he took it away from you; he kicked your ass and you got yourself arrested—very stupid, Tino. Now, guess what, your gun matches the one used to kill those girls. But it doesn't matter, Tino, we have an eyewitness who watched you murder every one of those girls … well, all but one."

"*Maldición*," said Tino. "It was that little *conejo* from Ixcán. I knew I should have…."

"Should have what, Tino?" asked Gabby.

"I knew she would be trouble, the *puta calle pequeña*. I should have shot her twice."

There it was—Tino Alvarez had just confessed.... Gabby looked at Tino, and then at Joe who held up his hand and shook his head.

"Tino, something is puzzling me. There are a dozen Harley Davidson dealers in Mexico and at least one I know of in Costa Rica: why did Señor Espinoza want you to take the risk of buying here in the States?"

Tino did not answer but instead said, "You no can slap me, señor, police here no can slap; I have rights."

At that, Joe reached out and slapped him with his other hand. "Look at me, Tino. I am not a policeman and I can do more than slap you, my friend. You know what I think, Tino? I think you were trying to beat your boss out of a motorcycle, eh amigo; you'll be lucky to not die in jail."

Tino looked at them both.

"Maybe we can make deal, no?"

"Now look at *me*, Tino," said Gabby. "You have one shot at this, Tino. If you lie to me again, or if you jerk us around for *un minuto*, you will see your last chance to live, walk out that door. We can save your life, Tino, but today only. Now, why don't you tell us a long story about what's really going on here?"

CHAPTER 13

Cozumel, Mexico

After a short layover in Dallas, Joe and Gabby got off the plane in Cozumel, Mexico, and breezed through customs with fresh passports identifying them as John and Anna Edgar from Camarillo, California. John was an industrial container salesman, and Anna was an administrative assistant for a small software company. They were finally getting to celebrate an overdue honeymoon, and you could tell by some of John's awkward behavior. It was his first marriage and Anna's second, but she was a very patient bride. It was their first time to travel to Latin America, and their excitement was evident as they enthusiastically perused dozens of travel brochures. They had three weeks of vacation and, as of yet, hadn't decided where all they would go. A driver met them at the airport holding a sign that read EDGAR. He would take them to their hotel and eventually brief them on the latest whereabouts of Juan Delmar Espinoza.

The FBI came in behind Joe and Gabby and cleaned up the mess with Tino Alvarez. He was arraigned in federal court, where nothing about terrorism was mentioned but where he understood a conviction for the murder of sixteen young girls would cost him his life. Because of the heinous nature of the crimes, there would be no press releases. Nor would there be any insinuation that a deal may be offered, granting him immunity from the death sentence. Currently, the US was fighting extradition requests from Mexico as well as Guatemala. To the great relief of Sheriff Culpepper, Tino was transferred from the Pima County Jail to a maximum-security federal penitentiary in Tucson. However, before they could guarantee his safety Tino had to sing, and sing he did. If ever Señor Espinoza stood trial, the testimony of Tino Alvarez—including the murders, drug deals, sex trafficking, and the bribes paid to both Mexican and US authorities—would ensure multiple convictions. Knowing Señor Espinoza would soon put a contract on his head, Tino was isolated and guarded around the clock. The agents from the Bureau were amused at his frequent questions about hanging prisoners in the United States. They figured whoever had lied to him had done them a favor, so they just let it hang... so to speak.

Both Joe and Gabby figured as soon as Señor Espinoza learned the fate of Tino he would be on the move. The horrific ordeal regarding the young Guatemalan girls had been the top story on every network, as had been the arrest of a suspect. It would have been nice to use Tino as bait, but that opportunity was long gone, so now it was time to allocate all the resources of the NSA.

Meanwhile, there was one thing Joe couldn't shake from his mind. Why would a man like Espinoza want Tino to buy those two bikes in the US, especially when Tino didn't have the information necessary to complete the transaction? Joe filed it away and decided he'd come back to that one later.

The person holding the sign at the airport was a fellow named Chad Longmire, but everyone called him Piper. He was a Midwest boy from Indiana and, for six years, had flown the infamous A-10 Warthogs in the US Air Force. He was a respected, badass pilot, who had flown missions in Afghanistan and Iraq. He was decorated twice for saving Marines and Army infantry pinned down by Taliban mortar and machine gun fire. Thinking it was time to make some money, he left the military and became a commercial pilot. He and United Airlines had a *"parting of the ways"* after several complaints from fellow pilots who said they would never fly with him again. Finally, Chad found a home with Mayan Air. They were a small but respectable Mexican airline, and Longmire loved flying the routes between Veracruz, Cancun, and Cozumel. The gig was working out perfectly until an incident involving an Italian swimsuit model, her poodle, and a disgruntled copilot. Apparently, Capitan Longmire persuaded the copilot to check the back of the plane and immediately seated the beautiful model in his place… along with her dog.

It would most likely have been overlooked, except he let her land the plane.

Unemployed for six months, Chad got a phone call that changed his life. His new partner offered him a sleek and fast Piper M600 and a job flying business associates in and out of questionable locations throughout Latin America. They would also throw in a Cessna 182 for those unexpected jungle and mountain excursions. The pay was nominal but the medical benefits were excellent and excitement was guaranteed. The only drawback was the three months of training as a communications specialist for his new employer, the Central Intelligence Agency.

Joe and Gabby liked him right away. There was chilled champagne in the back of his Range Rover and dinner reservations for the two of them at their hotel. It was important to maintain the ruse of their honeymoon.

"Folks call me Piper," he said. "Now, let's pop that champagne and get this honeymoon started."

The cork flew out the window and off the windshield of a passing taxi.

"Have a nice dinner, you two. I'll pick you up for coffee at 10:00 AM and we'll discuss your travel plans at my office. It's located inside the hangar back at the airport. There is a popular café next door, and they have excellent huevos rancheros."

CHAPTER 14

The Perfect Latte

As Mel walked from her reserved parking space at City Hall, she spotted the crowd and seriously considered returning to her car to drink her coffee in peace. There was quite a commotion next door at the county courthouse, but Mel took her coffee seriously and protected the time she carved out for her first latte of the morning. It was the one thing she could always count on to be consistent and perfect. Gringo Joe's Espresso was a favorite and frequent stop on her way to interview suspects, chide a grand jury into prosecuting, or when headed to court. Ever since a wild-abandon and irresponsible road trip, she had an incurable case of OCD—Obsessive Coffee Disorder. Six months earlier, when she'd first driven into Steelhead, Oregon, she didn't know the difference between a dark roasted espresso bean and chicken noodle soup. However, that was then and things had drastically changed. Michele Randle had become an unmistakable, certified coffee snob. The espresso shot had to be *pulled* fresh in the last fifteen seconds before the steamed milk was added. That was only the beginning. If dining in, the milk needed to be steamed to 150° F; if it was to go, 160°. And, of course, the all-important pour must be executed properly.

As you can imagine, for Mel, stopping for a tall double-shot, one-pump vanilla latte wasn't an exercise to be taken lightly—it was a religious experience. Mel was a sweetheart and adored by everyone on the right side of the law, but she was extremely good at her job and expected the same from others. If you couldn't or didn't do your job competently, you—and everyone else within earshot—would hear about it, including secretaries, court clerks, patrolmen, detectives, investigators, and, certainly, baristas. About the only thing that softened her perfectionistic nature was a perfectly made latte, and now her morning ritual was in jeopardy.

It was her experience that when there was a crowd outside the courthouse, it was usually drama best avoided. Rarely did it make a difference, and whoever was picketing, marching, boycotting, or voicing their dissatisfaction would get it off their chests and life would resume. However, today's crowd looked to have some staying power, and when someone yelled her name, it was too late to retreat. She strapped on a fake smile and walked into the fray. Lela, from the file room, was the first to approach her.

"What's going on?" asked Mel.

Lou Bailey, a longtime personality for Steelhead's oldest radio station, answered her question.

"It's Bill Crivelli, who else. He's called a press conference and is asking that Mayor Abercrombe resign and for Archie Anderson to be fired immediately. He's saying we've waited long enough and the mayor is guilty of cronyism, corruption, conspiracy, and one other word starting with a 'C' which escapes me right now."

"Oh, great, what kind of person pulls this crap just before Christmas? Any mention of me being a crony yet?"

"Not yet, Mel, but the morning is young."

By now a sizable crowd of city and county employees had gathered around her, as though waiting for orders.

"What should we do?" Lela asked.

Mel was five feet, four inches tall in her stockinged feet, but warranted the respect of her peers from day one. She took a sip of a rapidly cooling latte and said, "Well, let's charter a bus, go to Portland, and take in some sightseeing, maybe do the Homes on Parade tour."

Only Lela thought she was serious and said, "Really?"

"No!" snapped Mel. "How about we all go inside and do what we're getting paid for? This bozo is just trying to get another headline because he hasn't been in the news for almost a week now."

Mel headed toward her office, but not before she heard her name used in vain from the microphone of Mr. Crivelli.

"And speaking of illegitimate appointments, there goes Assistant District Attorney Randle, another one of the mayor's buddies."

She so wanted to walk back over and teach Bill Crivelli some judo, but instead yelled, "Merry Christmas, Bill!" warranting a chuckle from everyone, as the crowd dispersed, taking refuge from the cold drizzle.

For the past month, Mel had begun a file on the business practices and associates of Mr. Crivelli.

It wouldn't be long, she thought.

Mel had taken the Oregon bar exam and passed with ease. Some states allow reciprocity for attorneys to practice, but California is an exception. No one accepts the California Bar, nor does California allow attorneys licensed in any other state to practice without first taking and passing their own exam. It's as if California is another country instead of a member of the Union. The idea of the sovereign nation of California is discouraged by most, encouraged by some, and applauded wildly by Texas.

Regardless, her expenses were covered and Mel could legally practice Oregon Law. Archie Anderson, still fighting and defending himself from two frivolous lawsuits by Crivelli and friends, was a generous and honorable man. Officially he only worked ten hours a week, but spent another ten helping Mel get up to speed.

After completely straightening out Hobie Abecrombe's legal mess with the feds, she handled most of the prosecutory docket and still had time to dig into William "Bill" Crivelli's personal and professional dealings.

Sarah, Mel's admin assistant, buzzed her and said the mayor was on line one.

"Hello, Mayor. Tell me where you're hiding so I can join you."

Hobi laughed and said, "Absolutely not, they'll follow you and I'll have to answer all the same dad-gum questions again."

"It's all right, Hobie," said Mel. "I know you're out at the winery pining for a slice of Lizzie's quiche and probably some early eggnog."

"Dang it, Mel, if you tell anybody... I swear."

Mel laughed and asked what she could do.

"Mel, we have to get out in front of this thing with Crivelli and I was wondering if you'd make a statement. The reporters and TV crew are still lingering. They say they won't leave until they get a comment in response to Crivelli's accusations. Archie's too dang vulnerable and his legal counsel forbids him to say anything and I'm certainly not in the mood. What do you say, Counselor, want to take one for the team? I'll send over a cigarette and blindfold."

Mel chuckled and said she figured it was her turn. "I'll do it, Mayor, but I want to get my ducks in a row first."

"You mean you're headed to Joe's for some coffee."

"It won't hurt a darn thing, Mayor, and I hear Joe's back from one of his mysterious trips. I'd like to bounce a few things off him, if you don't mind?"

"Great idea, Counselor, I do it all the time. The guy has insight that I simply can't find anywhere else."

Mel called her pal, Lou, at the radio station. She "leaked" the idea she might make a statement on behalf of the mayor and the city of Steelhead around 4:30 PM. Her next call was to Joe.

"Hey there, stranger," she said as Joe answered his cell.

"Hey yourself. I was thinking it was about time for your second latte."

"My thoughts exactly. Any chance we could grab a corner table? I hate to bombard you but I have a bit of a situation and I need my spiritual advisor's insight."

"Be my pleasure, Mel, I've missed you."

"Ditto," she replied. "See you in about half an hour."

Since meeting Joe over a year earlier, their relationship had evolved. It was somewhere between best friends and the occasional short goodnight kiss. Like most everything else in each of their lives, it was complicated. While there was never any mention of a romantic commitment, there seemed to be an unspoken something-or-the-other lingering about. Mel was swamped, often burning the midnight oil, and Joe had this "other thing." He randomly took trips down South to check out a new blend of coffee. Mel didn't buy it, but whatever it was, she figured it was important and didn't ask too many questions. Regardless, she worried. She always assumed it had something to do with what he used to do in the military. She certainly knew there was more to Joe Chandler than coffee. Joe was naturally a reserved, introspective person. Nevertheless, he made it distinctly clear that he was grateful and blessed to have Mel in his life. And that was another thing; while almost no one else she knew used such words, Joe comfortably said things like blessings, grace and thankfulness. Churchy people say stuff like that, but with Joe it was different. It was natural and comfortable, as if it resonated from deep in his soul and he didn't need to guard himself from it. Several years earlier, Mel's faith in God had gotten filed under "small g" and buried beneath her ambitions. Anyway, while Joe was ruggedly handsome and fun, the idea that he lived for something or someone bigger than himself was refreshing. Before Joe left on one of his "coffee things," he always handed Mel a book that they would discuss over a nice dinner when he returned. The books were amazing and a wonderful escape from her hectic life, but it was the discussions she loved—Joe taking life's deepest mysteries and unpacking them with incredible word pictures and spellbinding stories. Often, as they talked late into the evening, she swore she could smell the salt and feel the sting of the windblown wave from the Sea of Galilee.

In the dark recesses of a nook, there was a table where those wishing to do so could hide behind their laptops or personal devices. While Gringo Joe's Espresso could be a very social place, especially during the holidays, sometimes folks needed to be alone with their coffee and the world outside of Steelhead. It was there where the two parked with their favorite drinks and today's special, a huge slice of zucchini-walnut and cinnamon apple bread.

"You sure know how to entice a girl, Joe Chandler."

"Yes, finding the world's best coffee beans and hiring Herr Elsa Müller to do our baking seems to lure in a steady stream of lovely, unsuspecting attorneys."

Mel glared at him for a moment, but they both smiled and thought how good to be back in one another's company.

"I'm glad you're back safe," she said, staring down at her cup. "I hope your coffee business wasn't too dangerous of a trip.."

Joe smiled and lowered his head. "What could be so important as to drag a lovely damsel over to our distressed side of the tracks?"

"I'm afraid the damsel might be in distress."

"Let me guess—Bill Crivelli?"

Mel told him about the press conference and asked his advice about how measured her response should be. She also mentioned that while he wouldn't admit it, Hobie was close to being scared and Archie was exhausted and about to throw in the towel.

"I've known those two men for almost twenty years. Both of them came out to the vineyard when I was still very young and did everything you can imagine to help my parents. Archie got my dad through some rough legal battles, one that almost cost us the entire farm. The Abercrombes loved to come out during harvest and pick grapes. One harvest, when we were short of labor, they showed up with a dozen friends, rolled up their sleeves, and picked grapes until midnight. That was a great year. We had a big bonfire and Jose played his guitar while Sonata and all the women danced around the fire. Leonard Tettleman brought over a barbeque trailer and grilled burgers and hotdogs."

Joe slipped away to a simpler time and Mel was swept away with him, but Diva's voice brought them both back to reality.

"Hey, girly girl, just wanted to say hi and see if I could bring you two another coffee?" She put two large ice waters on the table, and when they didn't answer, she quickly grabbed the empty dishes and eased away. "No worries, I'll check back in a bit."

Mel could see Joe's concern turning to anger as he considered the fate of his two good friends.

"I think it's time to give Mr. Crivelli a taste of his own tonic," Joe whispered. "As they say, the best defense is a good offense."

"My thoughts exactly; I've been doing a little digging and I have a file I'd like to share with you. I think our Mr. Crivelli and his friends are very ambitious and a little dangerous, and I really didn't want to take this one alone. I also think they have an agenda larger than some old, personal vendetta."

The two spent the next hour poring over the file and exchanging insight. Slowly patterns formed, twists were unraveled, and a mosaic, once dark and invisible, faded into the light.

CHAPTER 15

PIPER

At 10:15, Piper arrived at the hotel lobby where Joe and Gabby had been waiting for twenty minutes. They climbed in and both sat in the back.

"Good morning," Piper said. "How are the honeymooners today?"

Gabby, accustomed to punctuality, expressed a bit of disappointment with the driver. "I see you've adjusted to *estilo de vida relajado*, the laid-back life of Mexico, Señor Piper."

"Yes, I have, and I apologize for being late, but it's part of the gig. If I were early, I'd look like a US government employee. You guys hungry or want to get to work?"

"I can always eat," said Joe. "But watch out if the señorita orders buttermilk pancakes."

"I'll keep that in mind," said Piper as they sped off to the airport. The food was good and the place was crowded, so they kept the conversation very touristy. Once done, they drove down the street and pulled next to a guard shack where Piper said hello to a uniformed man who obviously knew him. The guard did a courtesy peek inside, glanced at the sticker on the window, and waved them through. Piper entered a six-digit code, opening another security gate, which gave them access to a restricted area. He unlocked a door and they walked into a large airplane hangar.

The two planes sat inside, fueled and ready to go at a moment's notice. There was an alarm system, and five security cameras on the walls and ceiling. The door to the office was sitting behind another chain-link fence where fuel and tools were stored.

"Goodness," said Gabby, "you sure are a paranoid tourist guide."

"Oh, it pays to be cautious, especially in my neighborhood."

Once inside the chain-linked gate, Piper opened a steel door, set in a double concrete block wall, turned on the lights, and they entered an office that looked more like an internet café. Along with several maps and satellite images, there was a blue neon Dos Equis beer light and some extraordinary aerial photos lining the walls.

"Impressive," said Joe. "I've seen shabbier command centers in the States."

"Yeah, it's true. Down here we don't get a lot of second chances, so they threw some money at this joint." He turned on a computer, opened the latest intel report, and gave it a quick read.

"Our sources in Costa Rica say that while Señor Espinoza is still in his villa, he has doubled his security detail and there is a great deal of people coming and going, so something is definitely up."

"If he's doubled his security, that's going to complicate matters," said Joe.

"Absolutely, and the last word I have from Pike is to stand by as the boys and girls over at NSA draw some conclusions. According to this report, one thing they have confirmed is several visits from a doctor."

"So, who's sick?" asked Gabby.

"Well, it says here the doctor is one Anna Munoz MD, the chief of oncology at a Catholic hospital in San Jose. It looks like while they can't confirm it as of yet, they believe Espinoza was at the same hospital for nine days, and it mentions several visits from Father Dominic Gonzalez."

Gabby made a silly face and a cynical comment about how weird it would be to find a priest at a Catholic hospital.

"I hear ya, Gabby, but in this case the priest is from Mexico and he happens to be the brother of Noella Espinoza."

"Excuse me?" asked Gabby. "But Noella—the wife of Señor Juan Delmar Espinoza?"

"The very same."

"Well, that's not a coincidence," added Joe. "Maybe our mission will be cut short and Señor Espinoza will do us all a favor and expire of natural causes."

"That's true, but in the meantime our orders are, and I quote, 'Stand down until advised.' So, while we're standing down, do either of you like to dive?"

Both Joe and Gabby looked up and smiled.

The next several days were spent in the exhausting service to their country. Joe and Gabby rented gear at the Blue Parrot Dive Shop and Piper met them at the dock in a beautiful forty-foot Rivolta. It was a magnificent boat powered by twin 480-hp Cummins diesel engines.

Once aboard and underway, Gabby shook her head. "You got to be kidding me; another perk of the job?"

Piper explained how certain toys, once owned by drug runners, often get confiscated. Fortunately, a few get new IDs and registration numbers and become the property and tools of the US government. This particular craft had been loaded with heroin and snagged by the coast guards in the Florida Keys.

Gabby rolled her eyes and said, "I got a cool sweatshirt and coffee mug about two years ago."

Piper laid his head back and laughed. "Want to drive?"

"Yes, I do. Just give me a heading and hang on to those Maui Jims."

A few days later all three of their phones lit up, advising them of a video teleconference at 0700 hours the following morning. Director Valenzuela's face appeared on a large monitor as the three of them sat at a table inside Piper's office.

"Gabby, you and Mr. Chandler look well, and apparently the sunshine is agreeing with you both. Hopefully you haven't been too bored with nothing to do but eat seafood, run up a healthy bar tab, and go scuba diving on the government's dime."

The two squirmed in their seats but said absolutely nothing. "That's the problem with sending good personnel down to Agent Longmire—they get fat and sunburned and I pay the bill."

Now it was Piper's turn to squirm as he stared down at his flip-flops. Piper would later tell Joe and Gabby it was the usual and expected reprimand, and he'd heard it a dozen times.

"I'll let Pike finish the briefing and I welcome each of you to interrupt if you have something to add."

"Good morning, troops. We have suspected for quite some time that either Señor Juan or possibly Señora Noella Espinoza could be seriously ill. We thought it might be the señora because the crime sprees didn't slow down and, in fact, they increased in frequency and the degree of violence. It didn't sound like the business practices of an unhealthy drug lord and, as you know, the incident with the girls from Guatemala was the crossing of the Rubicon for us. However, as of late yesterday evening, there have been some interesting developments. One of our senior diplomats at the embassy in Mexico City received an interesting phone call that we have now been able to authenticate. The call was from a priest named Father Dominic Gonzales, who lives and works in Guadalajara, Mexico. As it turns out, he is Señora Espinoza's brother, but from what we have been able to gather, he's an extremely well-thought-of leader within the archdiocese. There is no indication of corruption or collusion with the Espinoza drug empire whatsoever. Now, with that said, here's the twist—Father Gonzales told our man in Mexico City he would like to meet with a representative of the US government regarding his brother-in-law. And, just to get our attention, he informed us that Señor Espinoza has terminal pancreatic cancer and has been extremely sick for months. Furthermore, he said Espinoza has asked for absolution for his sins and, at the Monsignor's insistence, wants to, and I quote, 'clarify some things.'"

"What kind of things?" asked Gabby.

"That's what we asked, and were told the Espinoza Crime Syndicate had been hijacked by an American."

Pike wanted the information to sink in, so he didn't interrupt the silence.

"Holy guacamole," said Piper. "Do we believe him?"

"At this juncture we don't know what to believe, but we certainly want to hear the man out. We've scheduled a meeting with Father Gonzales and, Gabby, I want you all over this. The State Department insisted their liaison from Mexico City do the interview, but we got it nixed and right now it's all you. Longmire, I need you to give this mission your undivided attention. I want you loaded and in the air as soon as possible. There is a small private airfield near Lake Chapala. It's about twenty miles southwest of Guadalajara and we'll email you the coordinates as well as the address of the meeting. There are about five thousand gringos living in Chapala, so you shouldn't raise any eyebrows. We have a government contractor who retired there, and his villa is a secure meeting place. Okay, folks, any questions?"

"Col. Pike—excuse me, sir," said Joe. "If you don't mind, there are some things weighing on me that don't add up. For one, why would a man as smart as Espinoza ask some donkey like Tino Alvarez to stop in the US and buy him two Harley Davidson motorcycles? Especially since Alvarez didn't even have the registration information. Furthermore, with a dozen Harley dealers in Latin America, why take the chance if you just ordered the guy to kill seventeen girls? And, last but not least, what the heck would a man dying of pancreatic cancer want with two motorcycles? It seems to me he'd have a great deal more on his mind other than Harleys."

"That's a great question, Sergeant," said the director. "Since you've given it some thought, what's your take?"

"Sir, I'm not quite sure, but I would say it lends credence to the idea that maybe someone else might have been pulling the strings. It does seem plausible, sir, that Alvarez and whoever he's working with may have been using Señor Espinoza's reputation and money to indulge themselves. As far as the Harleys are concerned, sir, I think it was Tino's call. I sincerely believe the man saw an opportunity to snag himself a couple of Harleys. It just doesn't make sense to me that it came from Señor Espinosa."

"All right, I think we need to have another come-to-Jesus meeting with Tino Alvarez. Seems to me that maybe his loyalties are a bit confused, and it's possible he knows a hell of a lot more than the jerk is telling us. Gabby, I'll need a report on my desk right after that meeting."

Immediately, the monitor went blank and Piper whistled and said, "Holy guacamole!"

CHAPTER 16

North of Here, Inc.

It had taken Mel weeks to find it. While corporations are primarily used for tax and liability protection, they are also structured to hide the names of the people who actually own or benefit from the actions of the entity. While there may be layers of LLCs, S Corps, C Corps, and offshore shell corporations hiding the identities of corporate officers and board members, at the end of the day they're people, and those people have names. She probably would have missed it if not for a paper she had written during her final year of law school.

As assigned by her professor, she had to write a treatise defending a Washington DC physician who had grown clinical marijuana for his cancer patients. Pot certainly has a dark side, but it's a certified fact that it helps patients through the nausea and misery of chemotherapy. His crime was dispensing the drug three days prior to the passage of B21-0192, the Medical Marijuana Laboratory Testing Amendment Act of 2015.

As introduced, this bill gave the Department of Health the authority to establish independent testing laboratories to test medical marijuana and medical-marijuana-derived products. Because of this bill, the proponents of legalizing marijuana made the numerical sequence of **0192**, synonymous with pot, and that was what caught Mel's eye. Perhaps someone was trying to be cute or creative, but regardless, absorbed inside an IBC was a small corporation called, *"January 92 LLC"* or 0192 LLC. A few weeks earlier, while cleaning up some dead or suspended case files, she had come across an application to the Oregon Secretary of State. As stated by the applicant, the business class was real estate and land holdings. The name requested for the new corporation was *"January 92 LLC"* and it was signed by William Crivelli.

"What kind of land holding?" asked Joe.

"As best as I can figure, it appears that Mr. Crivelli has been buying or trying to buy Northern California and Southern Oregon farmland. He had either bought or tied up about 800 acres in Oregon when folks figured out they were sitting on Napa Valley north. Thanks in part to your parents, the valley exploded with wine fever, and the price of south-facing hillside property went through the roof. I think our pal, Bill, didn't wish to be too leveraged and started looking for partners. Less than two years ago, 0192 LLC got absorbed into an international business corporation called North of Here, Inc. So far, I have struck out on any of its board members, but I'm working on it. At first I thought they wanted to plant vineyards or go into the cattle business, but Bill's not a cowboy and they have yet to plant one vine. This whole thing just smells funny. Maybe it's nothing, but I'm betting that Crivelli and his pals are up to no good and trying desperately to hide it."

"Goodness, Mel, I'm surprised you have time to prosecute bad guys."

"Yeah, speaking of bad guys, I have to go get ready for a press conference."

"All right, in the meantime I think I'm going to do some poking around and make a couple of phone calls. If you're right, Mel, it sure looks like Crivelli and company want the mayor and our district attorney out of the way, and I may know why."

The press conference was short and to the point. The city attorney, Katie Sandburg, made a short statement about the city, standing by the mayor in this difficult time. It was very professional but Mel sensed that

Ms. Sandburg's statements and demeanor lacked conviction. She wondered if the city council lacked conviction as well. Mel decided to leave no doubt.

"Both the mayor and DA emphatically deny any wrongdoing and reject all claims by Bill Crivelli or any of his cronies. It's a waste of time and money on petty, unsubstantiated accusations and personal vendettas."

Then Mel decided to take Joe's advice and go on the offensive, as well as do a little fishing.

"Furthermore, both the mayor's and DA's offices are looking into independent counsel to sue for defamation of character. I know both of these men and the city and county are fortunate to have them. The same cannot be said for some of our inflammatory neighbors."

At that, Mel walked away from the microphones and cameras as reporters shouted questions. Realizing she was in an awkward position, Ms. Sandburg dodged a question about her role in defending the mayor and ran after Mel.

"Damn you, Randle! You put me in terrible position and left me to clean up your mess."

Mel stopped, glared directly into Katie's eyes. "Ms. Sandburg, if you mean in the position of doing your job and defending your boss, then yes, yes I did. However, in my short tenure here, I haven't seen you defend much of anything except your incompetence and, perhaps, trying to justify your affair with Deputy Dugan Brown. And my mess, as you call it, is me doing my job and showing loyalty to two good men."

Mel smiled and followed up. "And if any of your pals on the city council think they will get away with pitting you against me, perhaps you should think about another career … in another city. Good day, Ms. Sandburg."

"I'll have you to know Dugan and I are just friends."

Mel turned to find Parker Tackett had joined her as she headed for her office. Parker was on the City Council and had been loyal to both Hobie and Archie for years.

"Good Lord, Mel, remind me to stay on your good side and I hope I still am. That was one of the most impressive dressing-downs I've seen since the military."

"Councilman Tackett, if you or any of the council wishes to stay on my good side, why not show your friends some loyalty while their favorability ratings are down?"

"Hang on, Ms. Randle, I didn't come looking for a fight, and you were spot-on regarding Katie Sandburg. She smells a crisis and she's trying to decide which canoe to ride down the rapids. I, on the other hand, have never wavered in my loyalty to any of my friends. However, it's true Bill Crivelli has the ear of half of the council. Now, Mel, this business about suing Mr. Crivelli and his cronies, what in the world is that all about?"

"Yeah, about that, Parker, I have to admit I was a little mad, but I was also on a fishing expedition. I hope you and the council will allow me some latitude for a week or so. It will at least be interesting to see how Crivelli plays his hand and what other rats might crawl out into the light."

"I think I can appease the hoard for a week or so. Just tread lightly, Mel, and be careful."

The two parted company and Mel sat at her desk wondering if maybe she had played too weak of a hand on a bluff.

CHAPTER 17

Father Dominic Antonio Gonzalez Iglesias

Piper Longmire sat the M600 down smoothly on a short runway just north of Lake Chapala. There were a couple of hangars, what looked like an abandoned Quonset hut, and a new Mercedes G-Class SUV with a giant standing beside it. They were advised someone would meet them at the airstrip and take them to a villa. The someone was almost seven feet tall and had to weigh two-sixty.

"Look," said Piper as they were leaving the aircraft. "If that guy ever gets pissed, I want you to handle it—okay, Joe?"

They walked to the Mercedes where they were greeted by huge smile and warm handshake. The giant identified himself as Abebe. On the way to their accommodations, they learned Abebe was from Ethiopia and his name meant flourishing flower.

Piper, sitting in the back with Gabby, leaned close and whispered, "You better hope he's not interested in pollenating."

Gabby elbowed him and took in the scenery as they climbed into the hills. There was a security gate that Abebe opened with the push of several numbers. A large gate rolled away, revealing a warning sign about high voltage. A winding drive over the next hill brought them into an oasis with a large walled villa sitting in the middle. As the SUV rolled to a stop, there was a smiling, waving couple out front to welcome their guests.

"Hello, everyone, and welcome to our home! My name is Carol Anne and this is my husband, Ronnie Thibodeaux."

"Please," said Mr. Thibodeaux, in his extreme southern-Cajun accent. "Please, everyone, do leave your luggage; Abebe will see it gets to your rooms. Yolanda has made us all some pecan rolls, sweet tea, and lemonade. Ya'll come on out by the pool and let's do get acquainted."

Ronnie Thibodeaux had made millions of dollars in the natural gas industry. Because he was a huge donor, he was asked by a former president to serve as an ambassador to Mexico. As it turned out, Mexico held yet undiscovered, expansive pockets of natural gas. And as it also turned out, Ambassador Thibodeaux wasn't just another political appointee. Not only did he help Mexico with its gas exploration and make them billions of dollars, he convinced some powerful and influential people the US and Mexico should do all it could to curtail the flow of narcotics into America. He became a trusted liaison between the State Department and Mexican authorities. All the while, with his gifted and gracious wife at his side, he held parties and fiestas well attended by some of Latin America's richest and most dangerous drug lords. They were a friend to all and loved by everyone who fell under the spell of the Thibodeauxes. Thanks to him and his wife, informants were protected, corrupt officials and drug smugglers were arrested, and no one was ever the wiser. After retiring, Ronnie and Carol Anne Thibodeaux loved the climate of Chapala so much they built a home here, and felt it was their patriotic duty to continue to help in any way they could.

The following morning, after Yolanda's magical breakfast of buttermilk biscuits, scrambled eggs, bacon, fresh fruit, and freshly squeezed orange juice, a 1970s vintage Cadillac limousine arrived out front. It, too, was black and, while waxed and polished, it had certainly seen its share of Mexican highways. As Gabby stared through the plantation shutters, a driver opened the rear door and a tall and surprisingly handsome priest swung his legs and climbed out. He was dressed in a traditional black cassock with a white collar and what Gabby thought were expensive Italian loafers. Ronnie and Carol Anne were as welcoming as always.

"Monsignor, how absolutely wonderful to see you—please do come in and meet everyone."

After the introductions and a walk around the house and grounds, Carol Anne and Ronnie took their leave; after a large carafe of coffee and a pitcher of sweet tea were provided, Yolanda disappeared as well.

"It's quite a remarkable place, wouldn't you say?" asked Father Gonzalez.

Everyone chimed in and gave their kudos to the beautiful surroundings and gracious hospitality of their hosts. Then, there was a pause and all eyes were on the monsignor.

"I find myself in a position uncommon to men who have dedicated their lives to the church. However, my loyalties have always been with the sheep, and the shepherds must have compassion as Jesus had compassion. Don't you agree, Señor Edgar—that is your name, is it not?"

The priest's eyes were locked on Joe as he waited for a response. Joe, who had been staring at a beautiful painting, looked back at Father Dominic.

"A hired hand will run when he sees a wolf coming. He will abandon the sheep because they don't belong to him and he isn't their shepherd. And so the wolf attacks them and scatters the flock. He flees because he is a hired hand and cares nothing for the sheep."

The priest looked pleasantly surprised. He smiled, tilted his head, and added the next verses from John, Chapter 10 (NLT):

"I am the good shepherd; I know my own sheep, and they know me, just as my Father knows me and I know the Father. So I sacrifice my life for the sheep."

Again, it was quiet for a moment until Piper decided to break the mood.

"I'm wishing I had paid better attention in Sunday school."

Father Dominic laughed out loud and told Piper it was never too late.

At that, Piper looked down at his shoes. Again the priest spoke, but his mood was much more sullen.

"I am going to tell you some things I believe to be true; things from the lips of a dying man who cares very much about his soul. I know his history, I know the pain he has inflicted, and the evil things he has done. However, my sister, Señora Noella, has told me of other things. Almost a year ago, she began talking about a repentant man. Knowing my brother-in-law's history, I avoided seeing him, with the exception of a few holy days where he handed me a large check, as if to pay for his sins. This past Christmas, Juan pulled me aside and asked if I would hear his confession. I told him it might be more appropriate if heard by another priest. He said it would be harder to tell me, and he felt as if he should do the hard thing. I asked him when he would like to do it and he said it must be soon. That is when I found out about the cancer. Suddenly, we were loudly interrupted as his daughter, who came running in screaming 'Papa! Papa!' then grabbed his hand and begged him to come and dance with her.

"'How can a man refuse such a thing?' he said, and went to the party. Just after the celebration, Juan took his family to their home in Costa Rica. It was in the mountains, and they all loved it there. The only time he left was to go see Dr. Munoz, his oncologist in Guadalajara. Only his wife and four of his most trusted bodyguards were allowed to come. The children stayed with their nanny in Costa Rica. It was on one such visit for treatments when Juan learned his time was short, and I received the call from Noella. I arrived the next morning and Juan insisted that everyone leave the room and let him be alone with his priest. It was the first time he had ever called me that. Quite honestly, I was expecting a half-hearted confession from an arrogant monster, one who would offer God anything to heal him. What I got, instead, was a sincere and honest confession from a repentant man. After the confession, Juan looked at me and said he needed to tell me a story, and then he would ask for absolution and do whatever I asked of him. I agreed and was mesmerized as a story of murder, deceit, and betrayal unfolded. I thought as a priest in Mexico,

I had heard everything. However, during this conversation, I learned of monsters even more evil than my brother-in-law. I also learned once his enemies and competitors confirmed Señor Espinoza's illness, he became the old, crippled lion, running and hiding. Fortunately, he had a few loyal soldiers who vowed to protect him and his family. Juan began to hear of atrocities and crimes for which he was blamed, but knew nothing about. Finally, it was the terrible death of those young girls from Guatemala that made his decision for him."

"And what decision was that, Father Gonzales?" asked Gabby.

"He vowed he would begin to make restitution to the families and businesses he had hurt through his criminal activities. This is when he asked me to be an emissary between him and the families of the victims and when he asked me for absolution. I thought long and hard about this, about all the times Señor Espinoza had offered to write a check for his grievous sins and I told him it was not enough. I told him he must do everything in his power to stop those who had hijacked his empire and who would continue the work of Satan, the father of liars, rapists, murderers, and terrorists."

"What did he say?" asked Piper.

"He said it was too much. He said they would kill his family. However, I reminded him of the promise he had made to me on Christmas day, that whatever I asked of him for absolution, he promised to do."

"And now?" asked Gabby.

"We Catholics are superstitious people who believe certain saints, rituals, and even holidays are the same as God or His Son. It is a foolish mixture of pagan spiritualism and Christianity, which the Church has tolerated for a thousand years."

Father Gonzalez folded his hands in front of him, smiled, and continued.

"However, with over a billion Catholics in the world, sometimes we allow such things and turn a blind eye. One of the late Holy Sees suggested in a meeting with one of his cardinals, that a little fear, even though misguided, has helped keep order for a millennium. Isn't that right, ***Joe***?" Everyone's heads snapped up and looked at the priest.

"America is not the only intelligence service in the world. The Holy Catholic Church also has faithful eyes and ears, even in your government. Do not worry, my friends, your secrets are safe with me; I am a priest, no? Now, Ms. Mendez, you asked what is next—Señor Juan Espinoza wishes to speak with you and Mr. Chandler. He said if I believed you, if I trusted you, and you agreed to let him die at home with his family, he would give you a name."

"It would have to be a pretty big name, Monsignor, and I would certainly need to clear all this with my superiors."

There was quite a pause as everyone processed the information, as well as what just happened. Finally, to no one's surprise, Piper raised his hand.

"Excuse me, Father, but do you know my real name and what I do?"

"No, my son, I do not. However, I think it's time you came home. I have time for your confession before I leave."

Father Dominic looked at Joe and winked. Joe smiled but like the others, sat there with an uneasy feeling. They were thinking about all the work, the intelligence, and all the cloak and dagger stuff that had gone into this mission and, suddenly, their covers had been blown wide open by a Mexican priest. However, a good man, he thought—one they could trust.

"Well, goodness, Monsignor," said Gabby. "You have certainly given us pause, and perhaps someday we might discuss security breaches with you."

"Yes, perhaps, my child, but again you have nothing to worry about."

"I certainly mean no offense to you, Father Gonzales, but I do worry. These are exactly the kinds of well-intended leaks that get me and my team killed. Nevertheless, Monsignor, we do appreciate your discretion in the matter, and I want to applaud your courage and conviction. These men, not unlike your brother-in-law, Señor Espinoza, are responsible for hundreds if not thousands of murders, rapes, mutilations, and the kidnapping of innocent girls—little girls to be used as sex slaves. Most of these girls, Monsignor Gonzales, are, as you said, your sheep. Not unlike yourself, Father, I also see myself as a shepherd, and if I can get close enough, I will put a bullet in the heads of these wolves."

Joe could see Gabby's frustration intensifying and figured they had covered enough until they heard from Col. Pike.

"Thank you, Father Dominic. I agree with my partner, you have indeed given us pause. I guess our only question, since Señor Espinoza did ask, is how soon and where?"

"Yes, of course, my son. If your government will grant my brother-in-law immunity in exchange for certain information, and they will put it in writing, I will give you the email address of an attorney who will be expecting it. Afterwards, if you will call me at a number I will provide, I will arrange the meeting immediately."

They all stood and shook hands with the monsignor and started for the door. From seemingly nowhere, Ronnie Thibodeaux called from down a long hall.

"Ladies and gentlemen, Your Excellency, of course, you will be staying for lunch. Yolanda has prepared chicken and wild rice, I believe, Monsignor Gonzalez's favorite. Please, right this way to our garden room where we have prepared tables and seating to accommodate everyone. Monsignor, your driver is dining in the kitchen with Abebe and Yolanda. Please, everyone, right this way."

"My God," Piper whispered to Gabby. "I really wish that guy was my uncle."

The four guests joined Carol Anne and Ronnie for a magnificent lunch before seeing the monsignor out to his car. Of course, Carol Anne and Ronnie were waving furiously. Joe nudged Gabby and nodded toward Piper, who was smiling and waving just as furiously.

"I think he's looking to be adopted," whispered Gabby.

"We should probably be getting back," said Piper. "But I sure do love it here."

"Of course, you are all welcome to stay as long as you like," said Carol

Anne. "Honestly we don't have any plans, and ya'll are welcome to use the pool and tennis courts. We love to have guests."

"Boy, sounds good to me," said Piper, perhaps a bit too quickly.

However, Gabby made the decision for everyone. "You both must be a national treasure. Carol Anne, your home is stunning and all the more enjoyable thanks to your hospitality. We really do need to be going and if you could arrange transportation back to our plane, we would appreciate it."

"Of course, my dear, and on behalf of my husband and I, God bless you all, and thank you for your service to our great country."

CHAPTER 18

THE DIRECTOR

After Piper cleared the runway and got them airborne, he looked back to where Gabby and Joe had taken their seats.

"Holy guacamole," said Piper. "Talking about a game-changer."

Gabby looked at him and raised her eyebrows. "It's a pity," she said. "All these bullets and no one to shoot."

Joe looked at her a bit puzzled. "Really, Gabby, are you that disappointed that we may not have to kill someone?"

"Look, Joe," she snapped back. "I've been doing research, intel, planning, and field ops on this scumbag before you joined the military. I've seen what this sick bastard has done to innocent families and, yes, I am a little pissed that cancer is going to rob me of the chance to snuff out his worthless life. And by the way, Chandler, what was all that mumbo jumbo with the padre? I didn't see anything in your file about you studying to be a priest. I sure as hell hope you don't have a *'Jesus loves me'* moment when I need you to have my back with that Glock 19, okay?"

Joe looked out the window and decided it was best to let Gabby have her own moment. He understood how hard she had planned for a mission to kill a murderer, and now she may need to hold his hand as he died of cancer. Piper put them on the ground in Cozumel just under five hours from takeoff. Once the plane was stowed in the hangar and refueled, it was past dinnertime.

"Okay, you two, what's the plan? Are you going to sulk all night or shall we discuss our evening cuisine?"

"Look, I need a shower," said Gabby. "And then I need to wrap my head around this mess and get ready for a teleconference with the director tomorrow."

"Hey, no worries," said Piper, looking at Joe. "How about you, amigo? What say we go let off some steam, have a few beers, and let the boss sort this mess out; besides, tomorrow may never cometh."

Joe looked at Gabby, who still looked like she wanted to kill someone, then furrowed his brow and quoted Piper. "Tomorrow may never cometh?"

"Yeah," said Piper. "Isn't that a quote from the Bible?"

First Joe started chuckling and then Gabby, and when Joe erupted into bent-over laughter, both Gabby and Piper joined him and all three had a much-needed tears-running-down-their-face laugh.

When she could finally breathe again, Gabby looked at the two boys and said, "I need pizza and beer, how about you?"

They stayed out later than they should have, and Gabby probably had one too many. Piper, on the other hand, had several too many, and who knew you could do karaoke at a pizza parlor. Joe drove everyone back to the hotel and Piper crashed in his room. However, at 6:00 AM everyone's phone began dinging and buzzing, notifying them of a 7:00 AM teleconference. After picking up coffees—large coffees—they were present and accounted for as the screen came to life, and they saw Director Raphael Valenzuela's stern-looking face.

"What the hell's going on down there, Ms. Mendez? I expected a full report of your meeting with the monsignor on my desk this morning."

Gabby, completely aware she had blown off the report for a night out with the boys, started to apologize when Joe interrupted.

"Excuse me, sir, I'm afraid that is my fault."

Piper held his breath, thinking Joe was going to out him for the karaoke, and Gabby could only watch.

"And how exactly is it your fault, Sergeant Chandler?"

"Well, sir, actually it was a text I received from Father Dominic after we were airborne. He said he had some extremely pertinent information to our mission and would email it to me once he could confirm its authenticity. Thinking the information might have a great bearing on the report, I asked Ms. Mendez to delay it until this morning, sir."

"And?"

"Yes, sir, I just received the email from the monsignor en route to this location. It was encoded, sir, and Father Dominic said he would send the encryption key to a different email address."

At that moment, Gabby's phone buzzed, indicating an incoming email. She looked at Joe, who slightly raised his eyebrows, and she checked the message.

"Excuse me, Director," said Gabby. "It appears that I have received the inscription key."

"And you knew all about this, Ms. Mendez?"

Gabby didn't even hesitate. "Of course, sir, I am the lead on this mission. We were hoping to have everything resolved prior to this meeting."

"And you provided the priest with your contact information?"

"Yes, sir."

"And you provided Sergeant Chandler's as well?"

"No, sir. I believe the monsignor asked Joe for that directly. He and Joe got along very well talking about ... things, sir."

"What kind of things?"

"That is correct, sir," interrupted Joe. "We shared a common appreciation for Saint Thomas Aquinas and Saint Francis of Assisi, sir. It seemed appropriate at the time, and it appeared to break the ice. The monsignor asked if he could contact me again and refer a book, so I passed along an email, sir."

"A secure one I hope?"

"Yes, of course, sir."

Just as it appeared he might have a few more burrs up his butt, a man appeared in the screen whispering something in Director Valenzuela's ear.

"Very well," he said. "I have a call from the FBI in Tucson. I want a full report emailed through secure channels by 10:00 AM, is that understood?"

"Absolutely, Director," replied Gabby.

When the monitor cleared, Joe and Gabby looked at Piper, who indicated that the channel was indeed terminated.

"Holy guacamole, what just happened?"

"Yeah," said Gabby, staring at Joe. "What *did* just happen? I mean, besides covering my butt."

Joe explained that when he received the email from Father Dominic, he decided to wait and see if anything came of it. He told Gabby that he was aware that she was in charge, but he didn't want to make something out of nothing.

"It surprised me when I got the email. It seemed more personal at first than something mission-oriented. He asked about my education and if I had formal Bible training. I don't know, Gabby; after your tirade on the plane, I mean, well, you know, I wasn't exactly comfortable explaining myself. Then I got another email after we landed and never got the chance to fill you in. Like I said, I figured I would wait and see if anything came of it."

Gabby exhaled slowly as Piper nervously stared at her. "Okay, I get it. It makes total sense and I'm grateful that you jumped in when you did. However, I could have handled the director. It wouldn't have been the first time he came undone at my expense."

"You're right, Gabby, maybe I should have stayed out of it but I assumed we were a team and it seemed like the thing to do."

Gabby stared at him, thinking of the entire mess from the plane.

"All right, I need to clear the air right now. It wasn't you, Joe, and it certainly wasn't your interaction with the monsignor. In fact, I was impressed and thought your response was very appropriate. I was completely out of line yelling at you. And, you're right, we are a team and I had no business taking my frustration out on you. Please accept my apology."

"No apology necessary, Gabby, I totally understand and wouldn't have handled it near as well as you did."

"Me? You're the one who handled the director this morning. That was some fast-talking, Joe, and I really appreciate it."

"Hey, guys, all this mushy stuff makes me hungry. I think you make a lovely couple and should either smooch or fight while I go down to the cafe for food—what's everybody want?"

Piper saw the look in Gabby's eye and saw her clinch her fist and smile.

"On second thought, I'll just bring back a little of everything. I'll see you two in about an hour."

When the door slammed behind Piper, Joe laughed out loud. "I really think that decorated fly boy is scared of you."

"He better be," laughed Gabby. "But he does grow on you. I mean, in a junior high school sort of way."

They went to work on encrypting the email from Father Dominic and, as it turned out, it was a forwarded message from Señor Espinoza:

> *"My sources tell me that the cockroach named Tino Alvarez has betrayed me, and is associated with a longtime rival of mine, a man named Javier Rivera. My sources also tell me these men have been using my money and doing terrible things that would be laid at my door. This man lives in Tijuana, and has grown marijuana for twenty years. He is very rich and very dangerous. Tell the Americans that Rivera now works for an extremely dangerous man who is also a gringo, a very powerful gringo. I believe this man is responsible for the girls. He blamed me so that the gringos would kill me. Tell them we must talk soon. Tell them I will give them a name that will change everything. And to you, my dear priest, pray for my soul. My time is near. —Juan"*

"So what do you think, Gabby, do you buy it? Is it possible that this is all a ruse involving his brother-in-law, so Señor Espinoza can peacefully retire with his millions?"

"Wow, Joe, I think about that all the time, but I didn't expect to hear it from you. I certainly think he's capable of trying to pull something like that off. Imagine, he has us sent home and then receives a get-out-of-jail-free card from the US Attorney General. I'm afraid my attitude is extremely tainted, but we better get this to Langley ASAP and let them make the determination. But for the record, I think we need to go talk with Señor Espinoza and get a name. I mean, just in case, right?"

Gabby wrote the report and hit send just as Piper returned with food.

"Hey, kids, was there any kissing while I was gone?"

Gabby picked up a French fry and held it close to his face. "You know, Piper, at assassin school they taught us three different ways to kill a man with a French fry. Would you like to see one?"

Piper nervously smiled, handed her some catsup, and leaned close to Joe, "She didn't go to assassin school, right?"

"Actually, Piper, I'm not sure," whispered Joe, "but I'd keep my eye on that French fry."

After reading the report, Director Valenzuela sent a directive ordering Gabby's team to stand down. They were ordered to not leave the hangar and await evaluation from the chain of command.

"Pretty much well what I expected," said Gabby.

"We just undid about two years of planning and basically flushed several millions of dollars down the toilet. That is unless the new fish is bigger than the old one. Then we may need a bigger pole."

Piper glanced at Joe who tried his best to avoid eye contact.

"So, how long do you suppose the powers that be will keep us in limbo?" asked Joe.

"Well, if Señor Espinoza really is on his deathbed, then I figure not long. Right now, they are asking the attorney general's office to grant immunity to a dying man in exchange for information."

At 11:00 AM they got their answer.

"Pack you gear for a 0300 departure. Proceed to Zapopan Airport, ESE of Guadalajara, Mexico. You will receive your coordinates en route, and transportation will be provided by Monsignor Gonzalez. He will be the

intermediary for your meeting with Juan Espinoza. Immunity approved upon verification of information. Prelims have been forwarded to the law firm of BC&M as advised. PTKIP is approved. I repeat—PTKIP is approved."

Gabby showed the email to her team.

"It's been awhile, Gabby," said Piper. "But PTKIP—isn't that *permission to kill if provoked*?"

"Do you have a problem with that, Piper? Because if you do, you are welcome to stay with the plane."

"Negative," responded Piper. "I just wasn't figuring on a man dying of cancer pulling a gun, that's all."

"Good point," said Joe. "It's just in case this whole thing is some sort of a ruse, or we smell a rat. It's nice to know the agency's got our back and we can defend ourselves."

"PBP," said Gabby. "Typical DC protocol."

Piper had a puzzled look; he was lipping P-B-P, unable to place the acronym.

"Politics before people," said Gabby. "And you can synchronize your watch by that one."

Joe and Gabby walked over to the restaurant, did their tourist impersonation, and hailed a taxi back to the hotel. Piper offered but they decided to save him the drive. Besides, he was picking them up at 2:30 AM. During the cab ride, Gabby looked over at Joe and smiled.

"What?" he asked.

"I'm really glad you're here, Joe. I've done this a couple of times and the company wasn't always . . . well, you know."

Actually he didn't, and his mind was wandering, searching for context. Finally he decided it was a respect thing and thought it best to leave it at that. The cab pulled in front of the hotel, where several people were mingling in the lobby. They paid the driver, and when they stepped out Gabby grabbed his hand and whispered, "Don't forget, we're on our honeymoon."

Again, Joe's mind took off like a wild pig running from a jaguar. To protect their cover as newlyweds, they had gotten only one room but had asked for two beds. While checking in, Gabby had looked at the clerk and whispered that her husband snored. The lady had smiled and assured Gabby she understood. She made a comment referencing her own husband to a diesel truck without a muffler. By 9:00 PM, it was Gabby who was snoring as Joe lay awake, staring at the ceiling. He was thinking about the email from Father Dominic. In the first one, the personal one, the priest has told Joe that he sensed God's presence hovering over him, and that God would protect him while he was doing "*His*" work. "And," Father Dominic concluded, "you *are* doing God's work, my son."

Joe liked to wrap his mind around things, to kick them, flick them, and poke them with a stick until he was at peace with his actions. Because of the ever-changing matrix of this mission, there had been little peace. Joe wasn't Catholic and even took issue with much of Catholicism, but there was sincere comfort in Father Dominic's words, and Joe took great consolation in them and fell fast asleep.

CHAPTER 19

Tino

After parking at the Federal Correction Center in Tucson, Special Agent Irwin and his partner walked into the room where Tino Alvarez was seated. Slowly, he looked at a file and started shaking his head.

"Hmmm, well, that's too bad. Okay, Mr. Alvarez, since you haven't been very honest with us, our government has approved your extradition to Guatemala. Two military officers will be here on Friday to take you back for a hearing and whatever they do in Guatemala to extinguish vermin like you. Any question?"

Tino Alvarez stared at the agent with a puzzled look on his face.

"I no understand what you mean 'extinguish bermin.'"

"The word is 'vermin,' Señor Alvarez. It means insects, rodents, things that crawl around in the night, things that annoy you so you just reach down and...."

At that, Agent Irwin raised a thick manila file and loudly slapped the table where Tino was sitting. Tino jumped.

"And that's how you extinguish vermin, amigo. *Comprendo?*"

"I no want to go to Guatemala, señor."

"Well, you should have thought about all that before you lied to us and wasted our time." Special Agent Irwin stood, grabbed his file, and headed to the door.

"*Un momento, por favor, señor.* I am no sure what you want but I think maybe we make deal, okay?"

"No, Tino, no more deals. I don't want to listen to anymore crap from you and I've got a lot to do."

As they buzzed for the door to be opened, Tino Alvarez quietly whispered a name. He did so as though it scared him terribly.

"I'm sorry, what was that?"

"*Javier Rivera.*"

The two agents turned around and grabbed a chair.

"That's a good start, Tino; a very good start, but that's a name we already have, so you're going to have to do better. Tell me a story, Tino, and if it does not check out, I'm going to send your ass to Guatemala, and when they're done asking you questions, amigo, you'll beg them to shoot you. Now, where do we begin?"

CHAPTER 20

The NSA

The United States Foreign Intelligence Surveillance Court, usually referred to as FISA, is a US federal court established and authorized under the Foreign Intelligence Surveillance Act of 1978. Its primary job is to oversee requests from federal law enforcement and intelligence agencies, primarily for surveillance warrants against foreign spies inside the United States. Such requests are made most often by the National Security Agency (NSA) and the Federal Bureau of Investigation (FBI).

Since the murder of the sixteen young girls, the director of Latin American Affairs at Langley had asked for and received full cooperation from all necessary agencies for the apprehension of the perpetrators. Until recently, it had been a foregone conclusion the perpetrator was Juan Delmar Espinosa. Since Gabby and Joe's meeting with the monsignor, the now infamous email from Juan Espinoza, and the recent testimony of Tino Alvarez, there had been several high-level meetings. What had come from one of those meetings was a warrant from the FISA Court to wiretap an American.

The services of an Air Force Intelligence Analyst working at the NSA had been contracted to mine data, listen to conversations, and monitor emails of a man unfortunate enough to warrant such a thing. What he overheard redirected an entire investigation. The Air Force sergeant, like many of his peers, enjoyed playing video games to unwind from work. His favorites were RPGs or role-playing games, and his favorite RPG was *League of Legends*, also known as LOL. During an evening shift, he intercepted a call from his target to a semifamous hacker and Internet thug. It was a known fact this freakishly gifted hacker farmed out his talents to criminals. He was known only as Luther, and his name had surfaced in more than one investigation of drug cartels. The sergeant leaned forward in his government-issued office chair, and when a reference to Luther's favorite RPG game was mentioned, the sergeant confirmed he was recording the conversation.

"It's exactly the same as LOL, dude—you take on the role of a fictional character and you travel around with a group of other characters looking for wealth and adventure. In these adventures, you meet various monsters, and defeating them gives you money and experience points, which allow you to level up, learn new abilities, and purchase powerful tools. You know, like attacking Mexico. You use your abilities and tools to get rid of a monster, or to unleash the hoards from Langley. Then your boss does nice things for you."

"We'll get you your new toys, Luther, but we expect tremendous returns on our investments. This is only the beginning. Once we're done with Mexico and they're out of the market, we will own it and let our rich uncle pay for everything. You just keep me informed on our pal down south and the rest will fall into place."

"Listen, dude, I can tell you when the queen farts if you get me everything I asked for."

"It'll be at your warehouse on Wednesday and the rest is up to you. Oh, and Luther, trust me on this—don't double-cross this guy—he eats breakfast with the devil."

"No worries, dude, I got this and nobody will ever know a thing."

As ordered by Director Valenzuela, the target of the FISA warrant was an ex-government official who had worked for the Federal Drug Administration. His name was Lonnie Rudman, and Lonnie was an ambitious attorney. While at the FDA, he spent years trying to persuade the Federal Drug Enforcement Agency to reclassify marijuana from a class 1 to a class 2 drug. He was adamant the reclassification would clear the path to a more comprehensive policy reform that would liberate the medical community in its pursuit of research into marijuana. He and his cohorts came close, not being the first to try and relax the rules governing marijuana. Their efforts had greased the skids, and public sentiment was indeed relaxing. Rudman knew it would only be a matter of time. Still, for the moment the battle with the DEA was lost. The process was too tedious and directly tied to too many other agencies.

In order to affect change through the executive branch, a petition initiated from an outside party or from within the administration must be reviewed first by the Department of Health and Human Services by means of the Food and Drug Administration, and then by the attorney general who typically delegates the task to the Drug Enforcement Administration. If it weren't so stupid, it would be comical. Washington DC had evolved to a culture where change was destined to die the slow death of red tape. However, a certain bright attorney named Lonnie Rudman figured out Congressional rescheduling of a drug would be a much simpler process. If they chose to do so, Congress could amend the Controlled Substances Act to move cannabis to a Schedule II drug or off the schedules entirely. It could all be accomplished, decided Rudman, without going through the same administrative process that has caused many sane and savvy men to lose their minds and skip-naked through the halls of Congress. Regardless, because it is Washington DC, all such proposals had died in committee. However, in 2015 a bill called the Compassionate Access, Research Expansion, and Respect States Act garnered more attention than previous efforts in Congress. While it still hadn't happened, Rudman decided the congressional approach was, without question, the way forward.

Certain men and women have a drive that comes from deep recesses where most will never dare to wander. Some exit the womb with an unexplainable fire, and for others it was trauma or experiential. Several years earlier, Lonnie Rudman had watched his mother endure the ill effects of chemotherapy. He felt helpless and begged the medical community for anything that would relieve his mom's suffering. A doctor had told him new medical research in Europe was showing promising results from cannabis oils and the smoking or ingesting of marijuana. At the risk of losing his license to practice law, he bought some pot for his mother. The results weren't as dramatic as hoped, but it did provide some relief. While the experience set Rudman on a path of good intentions, the spirit-lords of the drug world are heavy task masters.

Three years ago, Lonnie Rudman's phone rang at his desk on the second floor of the Food and Drug Administration. A man told him he had watched his career with great interest and would like to offer him a better way forward. He said they shared similar goals and his team could use a talented attorney like Mr. Rudman. Lonnie had agreed to lunch and then to another and, finally, to a better way forward.

The intention was, that wiretapping this once mid-level government official would lead to the name of a much more important government official. However, by the time Lonnie Rudman terminated the call with Luther, no other names were mentioned. The intel analyst stopped the recording and called the agency to which he had been contracted. The call was rerouted to an office two floors above the sergeant. Col. Pike told the young sergeant to forward the recording via secure channels to his office. Within twenty minutes a meeting between multiple agencies was scheduled, and surveillance was arranged for Mr. Rudman. FBI agents and CIA field operatives were redirected to stay ahead of a fluid mission, now on both sides of the border.

CHAPTER 21

California–Mexico Border

A senior CIA field agent named Paul Ruiz stationed in San Diego, California, owned —as a cover—Lupe's Tile Store, a shop specializing in Mexican floor tile. He and his staff sold just enough tiles to warrant frequent trips back to Mexico. A remote warehouse located on a US Marine Corps Air Station in Miramar, California, was overflowing with Mexican tiles purchased from the small, retail shop. Lupe decided to retire when Paul showed up with a fat checkbook offering to buy her business. The CIA kept the name.

Paul's old Jeep Cherokee was parked on a hill where he was taking pictures with a very good camera and telephoto lens. It almost disappeared in the desert, but a satellite had captured images of hundreds of acres of black netting, hiding and protecting a gigantic marijuana farm from aerial photos and sunburn. This one belonged to Señor Javier Rivera.

Importing marijuana to the US has been a billion-dollar industry, but the fledgling legalization of pot for recreational use and its probable explosion for medical use was threatening the profits of wealthy Mexican drug lords. Suddenly the gringos were growing their own, and theirs was better. Mexican marijuana had been the gold standard for US pot smokers for decades. However, in the new world of legal markets and gourmet weed, aficionados were looking to the Americans for the good stuff. Like all industries, if you get complacent and do not stay ahead of the changing demands of the market, someone else will. It was in the illegal basements and the hidden farms in Northern California, Oregon, and places like the Ouachita Mountains of Arkansas, where new potent strains of pot were cultivated. Instead of twenty-dollar bags of Acapulco Gold, pot smokers were seeking out high-potency boutique pot from the US selling for hundreds of dollars an ounce, and this was making some folks in Mexico very nervous. One of those people was Javier Rivera, and Señor Rivera was trying to reestablish himself as the "King of Pot" and it wasn't working. He could not reproduce the strains the market was demanding and, subsequently, lost his American distribution chain to competition. That is, until he was invited to a meeting with a very powerful gringo. The only thing better than having an entire police force in your pocket was having an American politician with dozens of powerful friends. Javier Rivera could not believe his good fortune. A powerful, greedy American needed an experienced, ruthless Mexican as a partner. Javier concluded this was a blessing from Isidore and Maria, patron saints of farmers, and vowed to give generously to a local Catholic church; however, the charitable attitude passed and life for Javier continued as usual.

As a preliminary show of goodwill, Señor Rivera's new partner thought it would be a good idea to rid themselves of competition. He called it "thinning the herd." The gringo suggested they start with Señor Juan Delmar Espinoza. When Javier heard the details of the plan and was introduced to a traitor named Tino Alvarez, he began to question his good fortune. In fact, his courage weakened and he begged for a way out. One day, two friends of the American paid him a visit and he found his courage again—however, there would never again be a peaceful night's sleep ... ever.

Paul knew a man who had a son. The man had been a barber in Tijuana for thirty years, but when his son went to work for Señor Rivera, he didn't need to be a barber anymore and he retired. Paul had befriended the man and used to bring him boxes of leftover tiles so the man could sell them and make some extra money. When Paul stopped at the man's new home, the man came out to greet his friend.

"Señor, so good to see you again; come, sit on the porch and let's have a *cerveza*, eh?"

Paul, only known to the man as "*jefe*," smiled and took a seat.

"You have a very nice place, my friend. It is hard to believe haircuts and tile could serve a man so well."

He was a proud man but he knew it was no good to lie to his friend.

"My son, Benito, has a very good job and occasionally helps his mother and me. I tell him to keep his money but he insists that he has plenty and makes us take it. We are very proud of him." The man looked at Paul with a big smile.

"Do you know what your son does, amigo? Do you know where a young man with so little of an education makes so much money?"

Suddenly the man stopped smiling and looked at Paul. The pride that had been there moments earlier was replaced by fear—fear that was very evident in his eyes. It was as if the truth, pushing stubbornly at the door of his mind, had finally broken through.

"I don't think we should talk anymore, *jefe*. I don't think I like you no more."

Paul reached into his shirt pocket and pulled out a picture of two young men. They were loading large bales of marijuana into a forty-foot trailer.

"Listen, my friend, you have a very nice home and there is no reason you and your wife should not enjoy your retirement. You are an honest man who has worked hard—you earned it."

The man was very nervous but he was listening.

"Your son works for a dangerous man, a man that does terrible things to people who betray him. Do you understand, amigo?"

The old man nodded, his shoulders drooping and tears forming in his eyes.

"Listen, my old friend. I need some information from your son. I need a name and maybe I'll need him to take a picture—that is all. I am afraid it is the price for our secret. Do you understand?"

Again the man nodded.

"I need to speak with your son very soon. Here is the address in Chula Vista and the time I need him to come. It is a Sunday and it's his day off. He goes there to see a girl, so I know he can cross the border without any problems. You need to make sure he comes, so I can continue to protect you. I want to do this for you."

Paul stood and handed the old man the picture of his son.

"Make sure he comes: it is very important."

As Paul drove away, the man's wife came out of the house and found her husband weeping.

She sat down beside him and said, "*Siempre sabíamos*—we always knew." And then they held one another and cried.

Lying to people, deceiving them, turning spies into informants or drug dealers into spies—it was a very nasty business, but people like Paul Ruiz did it very well, and they saved American lives.

There were three additional agents watching the *taqueria* in Chula Vista, California, when Benito Castro strolled up to the window. As instructed, he ordered a couple of tacos and sat next to a man and woman sitting outside, wearing San Diego Padres hats.

"I like your father very much, Bennie, and you have put him into a very bad position."

"No, señor, it is you who has put me into a very bad position. You should have come to me and not told my father anything. You have broken his heart. He did not need to know. No, señor, you have done this."

The woman, a frequent partner of Paul's, looked at the young man, grabbed his hand, and held it very gently. She was very pretty and he did not mind.

"Listen, *mijo*. Every day people like Señor Rivera take good men—strong young men—and make fools out of them. He not only owns you, *mijo*, he owns your family and your soul. This man has murdered dozens of young boys exactly like you. Their bodies lie buried in the hills, because they either stole a little pot or wanted to quit. You work for an evil man, Bennie, and no one walks away alive. But today, Bennie, you are the lucky one. Because you have such a nice mother and father who don't deserve this heartbreak, we are going to give you, and them, a second chance. Do you understand, Benito? If you do this for us, we will see that your parents are cared for and we are going to help you get an education and a job—an honest job."

Bennie looked at them both. "I made a mistake and I am scared. I want out but I know he will kill me. I don't think you can protect me. He is a very bad man."

"Listen, Bennie," said Paul. "Have you ever seen any Americans come to Señor Rivera's business? Bennie, this is very important and we need your help. This is what we need from you, to protect you and your family. Has there been Americans, Benito?"

"Yes, there are two gringos who come about once a month. I think they are very dangerous."

"Yes, they are extremely dangerous and we need to know who they are. We need either a name or a photo. Have you ever heard a name, Bennie?"

"No, señor, no names but I would recognize them. I have seen them maybe two times."

Paul handed him a small paper sack. There were some inexpensive gifts for his parents and a very small camera. He instructed Benito on how to use it and told him how to contact him. Then he told the young man he should eat his tacos and wait a few minutes before he left, and then they were gone.

CHAPTER 22

SEÑOR JUAN DELMAR ESPINOZA

The plane taxied to a designated building a hundred yards from the end of the runway. There was a 1970s vintage Cadillac Limousine waiting. The driver looked familiar. When the plane was secured and luggage was unloaded, the driver came to greet them and to help with their bags. A rear window was lowered; Father Dominic Antonio Gonzalez Iglesias showed his smiling face. Once the luggage was loaded, the driver opened a rear door, revealing two large seats facing each other.

"Joe, my son, come and sit beside me."

Gabby and Piper sat across from the two and stared like strangers on a Greyhound bus. Father Dominic reached into a satchel, pulled out a leather-bound book, and handed it to Joe.

"I wanted you to have this. I have an extra copy and it is a favorite of mine."

Joe took the small book and read the title out loud, "*Aquinas Prayer Book: The Prayers and Hymns of St. Thomas Aquinas.* This is very kind of you, Monsignor; I don't know what to say."

"It is nothing, Joe, only a simple token of gratitude, and I give it to you knowing it will not be wasted." Father Gonzalez looked to the others and unapologetically said, "I did not bring any more copies of the book because I didn't think such things would interest you. However, let's discuss the matters at hand. Do you have any questions?"

"A couple, if you don't mind, Monsignor," said Gabby. "Can you please tell us about the facility where we are going and what we are to expect?"

"Ah, yes, of course; the ever vigilant shepherd of her flock. Always wise in your business, I presume."

Joe felt the tension between the two and interceded.

"Yes, Father Dominic, it *is* her job to keep us all safe, and she *is* very good at her job."

"Of course, I meant no disrespect, Ms. Mendez. We are going to a residence very close to the hospital, which is now owned by my sister, Señora Noella Espinoza. Many of their personal things have been brought there to make Juan comfortable. He purchased the home three months ago, made a few upgrades, and added a bit of security. Once my brother-in-law has passed, it is his wish for the home to become a sanctuary for the families of cancer patients. Noella and the children will not be present—only Señor Juan, an elderly servant named Rosa, and two of his security detail. The two men will be downstairs during our meeting. Juan knows you will be armed, as is his security detail. Ms. Mendez, I know you have great hatred for my brother-in-law and while it will be difficult, I ask, as a personal favor to me, that you try to be respectful. Señor Juan is very weak, only a shell of the man he was a year ago. If you will be patient, he will answer all your questions. Is this agreeable to you, Ms. Mendez?"

Gabby nodded and said nothing else until they arrived, then her gaze narrowed as she looked at Joe and Piper.

"Piper, I want you to stay outside the room, near the top of the stairs, and keep your eyes open. As soon as we go inside, I want to know where all the exits are. Joe, you and Piper take a quick look around and meet me back in the foyer. I want you both locked and loaded and I don't want any crap from the two goons protecting Espinoza—any questions?"

Gabby looked directly at Father Gonzalez. She was in operation mode and all pretenses were gone.

"All right then, Monsignor—your show, let's go."

The two security guards looked like men who knew their business. They were middle-aged, well-dressed, and wore dark sunglasses. They nodded at the monsignor when everyone entered and glared at the rest. Without hesitation, Joe asked the two men to show him and Piper the layout of the bottom floor. His Spanish was flawless and they looked at him as if making sure he was a gringo.

"There is no problem, señor: we have checked the house and it is fine."

With a bit of a firmer voice but still with a smile on his face, Joe looked back at the man. "*Eso es muy bueno, mi amigo,* but we need to see it with or without you, and we *are* in a bit of a hurry."

The man looked at Joe, hesitated, and then motioned for Joe to follow him. They were gone for less than two minutes and returned, then Joe briefed Gabby.

"There is only one exit door in the rear. It leads to a carport and then there is a walkway leading back to the front of the house. There is no alley and I did not see a line of sight into the upstairs from anywhere higher than ground level. There were no vehicles visible, and we checked all the closets and pantry. There was only the woman, Rosa, sitting at a small table in the kitchen. We were told there is not a basement." Then looking back to the Mexican, "And this man appears to be very competent."

Gabby looked at the two Hispanic men and said, also in perfect Spanish, "One of you needs to guard the backdoor and one the front. If anyone comes in the direction of this house, I want to know immediately—do you understand?"

It was obvious these men were not used to being told what to do, especially by a woman.

"Listen, señorita, I have been guarding *el jefe* for ten years. I do not need some *muchacha Americana* telling me how to do my job, *entender*?"

"*Por favor,*" said Father Gonzalez, looking at the man. "No problems for the Americans. Please, my son, they are here doing their job just as you are, no? They are my guests, so let us be respectful."

The Mexican looked at Gabby and grinned. "*Si, Padre;* for you I will do as you ask."

Joe, Piper, and Gabby followed Father Gonzalez upstairs. Piper stepped down the hall to the right as Joe and Gabby turned left, following the monsignor into a bedroom. Piper, who was generally a laid-back sort, was feeling uneasy from the drama downstairs. He slipped into a shadow and pulled the Beretta M9 from inside his waistband. He made sure a round was chambered, the safety was off, and located the extra clip in his jacket pocket.

They walked into a large bedroom that had a comfortable sitting area brightened by a beautiful bay window. There was an expensive leather sofa and several matching club chairs. Señor Espinoza was standing next to a recliner that had been arranged so that he might sit and look out the window. He was wearing some tasteful pajamas covered by a silk robe and adorned a colorful cravat around his neck. Nevertheless, there was very little life left in this man. He was desperately thin, his skin was ashen, and yet he stood erect and tried his best to make his visitors unashamed for him.

"Please come and be seated, everyone. Forgive my inability to entertain as you deserve, but I am afraid that today this is the best I can manage."

Father Gonzalez and Gabby sat while Joe remained standing near the window.

"I have asked Rosa to bring us some refreshments. Nothing special, but her lemonade is exceptional. Tony, it is so good of you to come."

Turning to Gabby, Juan explained, "I still call him Tony because that is what everyone called him when he was a boy. Dominic Antonio Gonzalez Iglesias, a big name for such a small boy, no? However, I knew he would be a great man one day, and we are all very proud of him. Such is the difference: I attained power and wealth and it destroyed me, and yet Tony here, he chose a life of abstention and it made him a saint. I did not always understand but now I do. The good Father here read to me the words of Jesus on his last visit:

'For whoever wants to save their life will lose it, but whoever loses their life for me will save it.' Correct, Monsignor?"

"That is correct, Juan."

"I wasted my life, and now I am very ashamed." Looking at Gabby, he said, "Life is not fair, *mujer joven,* but we must learn or we die as fools. Life has robbed you of the opportunity to bring me to justice, to pay society for my sins. Listen, señorita, no amount of money, no jail, no suffering, or even my execution, would have been enough. Please, forgive me.

"However, all is not lost: you came for some information, a man's name, and I will not disappoint you.

"When your country began legalizing marijuana, I knew it would change everything. Smuggling a few pounds of pot across the border near Nogales is how I began my career. Fortunately, I made several thousands of dollars before a *federale* working at the border discovered what was in my trunk. He pulled me aside and asked me if it was my first time to be caught. I told him it was. He explained the *dinero ciego—the blind money*—to me. Every time I came to the border, I was to ask for him and bring enough money to make him blind. Then, señorita, I understood how things in the world were done. I made a million dollars smuggling marijuana but it was hard work and it stunk. So I began dealing in other commodities that were easier and paid a great deal more."

Gabby shifted in her chair and said quietly, "Yes, like young girls."

"Yes, occasionally, like young girls. I was a businessman, and rich, powerful Americans were willing to pay a great deal of money. I am more ashamed of this than anything else I did. I told God the cancer was a small price to pay for what I had done to all those families. It is not enough, but for all who can be identified, Noella will see that they receive restitution. My wife will make it her life's work to atone for mine."

Father Gonzalez looked at Gabby and then over at Joe, who was listening intently by the window.

"Juan knows the money is not a replacement for their daughters, and, unlike what many who call themselves shepherds teach, money can never pay for sins. However, it is something, and it was his idea."

Again, Juan talked of the drug industry.

"When your state governments began to pass legislation to legalize marijuana for medical purposes, I knew it would only be a matter of time before powerful Americans began to fight over control of this new market. It will be years before the demands can be met by small, local growers. In the meantime, there will be billions of dollars made. Those who control the government contracts and meet the eminence needs of medical and the legal recreational users will become very rich. And, as always, it will be done by people who know people, especially in Washington DC."

"And you mentioned that you had the name of such a man. Perhaps one who would commit terrible atrocities to gain such power?"

Piper heard the footsteps of someone coming up the stairs and glanced around the corner. The security guard with the attitude was carrying a large tray of five glasses and a large pitcher of something. Piper quickly walked down to the doorway where everyone was gathered. "Are we expecting refreshments?"

"Yes; finally," said Señor Espinoza. "I am getting weary and some of Rosa's lemonade will be just what we all need."

Piper returned to see the man struggling as he topped the stairs and asked if he could be of assistance. The man did not answer but looked nervous, and only shook his head. When the man turned into the doorway, Señor Espinoza looked a little surprised.

"Rodrigo, what happened to Rosa?"

Rodrigo appeared to trip and almost threw the tray, which went flying in the direction of the couch. Before Joe could retrieve his weapon, Rodrigo had pulled a Beretta submachine gun that was hidden under the tray. The first burst of fire went through the middle of Juan Espinoza's face. The second was directed toward the large bay window, which exploded in shards of glass. Rodrigo sprayed one last burst in the direction of Joe, then ran and jumped, in a crouched position, through the window. However, the man was dead before he hit the ground. Everything happened in less than five seconds, but in the last second of those five, Joe had turned and hit Rodrigo in the back of the head with a double tap from his Glock 19. Suddenly, Gabby—who had instinctively pulled Father Gonzalez to the floor and covered his body with hers—began giving orders.

"Piper, downstairs! I'm right behind you. Joe, the shooter?"

"Shooter's down. Go, I got your six."

Piper dove around the corner to the landing at the top of the stairs. Machine gun fire erupted from the bottom, spraying the wall just above his head.

"Move!" yelled Gabby and fired around the corner as Piper jumped and rolled down the hallway. There was another burst of fire from below, then two quick taps, the sound of glass breaking, and then quiet.

"Clear!" Joe yelled from below. He had jumped from the upstairs window, landed on Rodrigo's dead body, and ran to the front of the house where he neutralized the second shooter. It was a mess, and to make things worse, there were sirens—a lot of sirens.

Gabby, with adrenaline still coursing through her body, was still giving orders.

"Joe, you get the priest! Piper and I will secure the bottom floor." Gabby held her Sig P-226 in ready position and took a quick look around. Rosa had been struck on the head, duct-taped and stuck in the pantry, but she was alive. Gabby yelled clear as did Piper, then she grabbed her phone and dialed a stored number.

When the police entered the building, their AR-15s were locked, loaded, and pointed at the Americans. Joe, Gabby, and Father Dominic were sitting on the stairs and Piper was looking after Rosa at the kitchen table. Their guns were laid in front of them and their IDs were in their hands, held over their heads. The American agents were there without permission, which wasn't unusual, but getting caught in a gunfight with dead bodies lying around was.

Things were extremely tense until a colonel with the Policía Federal arrived. Fortunately, he knew Father Dominic, but unfortunately, he did not know the gringos with the guns. There were a lot of questions, a great deal of explaining, and then there were more questions and some yelling. Finally, Father Dominic pulled the colonel aside and made a suggestion.

"It appears, Colonel Munoz, that under your command the police force has apprehended the famous drug lord, Señor Juan Delmar Espinoza. Unfortunately, Señor Espinoza and two of his bodyguards were killed during the intense firefight. And while it was a joint effort with the US government, the Americans played little role in the operation."

The colonel tilted his head and smiled at the monsignor. "Father Dominic, you are a sly coyote. However, perhaps you are right: I would probably get a promotion."

"Yes, my son, and perhaps your name and picture will appear in *El Informador.*"

"It is tempting, Father, but it would be most difficult to pull off, even for me. Americans with guns, on Mexican soil—this is a serious matter."

"Yes, Colonel, but you and I both know the Americans will be happy to pay a handsome fine and have this matter resolved privately. I think when you present your idea to the *commandante* it might go well with you, my friend. Besides, these *Americanos* saved my life; surely Mexico will be grateful, no?"

To no one's great surprise, a picture of Colonel Luiz Munoz appeared in all the Guadalajara newspapers and, of course, there were several TV appearances. After their guns were confiscated and a sizeable fine was paid, the colonel personally escorted the three back to their plane.

"It is a most *supremo* aircraft, *amigos*, and it was only because of my insistence that you are able to keep it."

Gabby looked at the colonel and smiled. "Of course we are very grateful, Colonel. Let us join the other well-wishers in congratulating you on your daring apprehension of such a dangerous criminal. And, perhaps if you discover the name of a gringo who is so powerful as to convince loyal men to kill their *jefe*, you will let us know."

"Of course I have no knowledge of such things, my friends, but in Mexico just like in America, if you have enough *dinero*, having a dying man killed is not so difficult."

The colonel handed Gabby a small piece of luggage. "A going-away gift for you; after all, I did get a promotion. *Adios, amigos.*"

CHAPTER 23

THE ESCAPE

As Piper was taxiing out to the runway, Gabby unzipped the bag as she and Joe looked inside. They pulled out their pistols and laughed.

"He kept the bullets," said Gabby. "Oh, well, no one to shoot, eh, Joe?"

"Not yet, Gabby, but I plan to reload—you?"

The last item in the bag was a book, *The Aquinas Prayer Book: The Prayers and Hymns of St. Thomas Aquinas.*

Gabby smiled and yelled out to Piper, "Well, Agent Chad Longmire! I think everyone in Mexico knows your name now—what do you think the Agency will do with you?"

Piper lifted the M600 off the ground so smoothly and quietly they hardly knew they were airborne.

"Yeah, good question, Gabby. I'm not a great saver, so I've been thinking about that. I figure I could always get a job smuggling pot across the border. It looks to pay better than Uncle Sam."

"Piper, you're a pretty boy and I don't think you'd fare well in a Mexican prison."

"Hear that, Mr. Edgar, she thinks I'm pretty. You better watch out, *amigo*, or I'll steal your wife."

They enjoyed a good laugh, knowing there wouldn't be much to celebrate in the days ahead.

Langley instructed Piper to immediately secure the facility at Cozumel. The boat and bush plane were already on their way to another facility in Nicaragua. They were specifically told which computers and communication equipment to grab, and then fly the M600 back to American soil before the Mexicans changed their minds. It was almost five hours of flight time to the hangar, and while Joe and Gabby grabbed computers, Piper disconnected radios and sensitive communication equipment. They shredded papers and Piper grabbed a few clothes, his old flight jacket, and took all the pictures off the walls. He also phoned a friend who promised to forward his vinyl record collection and take good care of his black cockatiel named Barry. Gabby ran to the restaurant and ordered a dozen tacos to go and three large orders of fries while Piper and Joe refueled the plane. They threw a case of bottled water, several more guns, and some ammo, in the cargo hold and taxied out. Langley had already filed their flight plan and, catching a good tailwind, they soon landed in Florida. They were exhausted and received permission to refuel and spend the night at the Naval Air Station in Jacksonville.

A Naval reserve pilot who was working as the OD secured them in three empty rooms next to the officer's club.

"Does anyone else need a beer?" asked Piper.

"Yeah, good idea," said Gabby. "It's certainly been a memorable day and I know we're all tired, but we should definitely decompress, don't you think, Joe?"

"Probably a good idea. I'd like to know what to expect at the inquisition, if you don't mind, Gabby."

Piper bought the two Coronas and a coffee for Joe to the table. Everyone took a deep breath and sat for several minutes in silence. Gabby spoke first.

"First of all, I've gone over it in my head a dozen times and I absolutely cannot take issue with anything we did. Piper, you asked the right question and there was no way of knowing what Rodrigo was doing."

"I should have," said Joe. "I caught a real bad vibe from the guy. I should have known when he walked in, but I hesitated."

"Look, Joe, we all need to be on the same page and that's not what I saw."

"Nor I," responded Piper. "If anything I should have tackled him when he pulled the gun, but look, Joe, the whole thing happened in a few seconds. They had it planned. Rodrigo was going out the window and his pal would keep us pinned down. I say we're damned lucky to be alive."

"Yeah, it did happen fast, but I won't make that mistake again."

"It was all instinct and reaction. I don't even remember grabbing Father Dominic and throwing him to the floor. When I looked up, I saw Joe spin and pop off two rounds, then, when I looked at the monsignor, he was staring at the barrel of my SIG and praying."

"Did anybody get a chance to thank him?" asked Piper. "I'm almost positive he spun the entire story for Colonel Munoz. I watched them for a long time and the *padre* was doing most of the talking."

"That's right," said Joe. "Right after that conversation is when the colonel pulled us all together and told us if we wanted to stay out of prison to keep our mouths shut and let him do the talking."

"Can you imagine a Mexican prison?" asked Gabby. "Two days in that holding cell and I was sure I was going to be eaten by rats."

"I think we all owe Father Gonzalez a debt of gratitude. I plan to write him and tell him how grateful we all are, unless anyone has an objection."

"You mean, like a letter?" asked Piper. "Do people still do that sort of thing?"

"Yeah, crazy, huh, but I actually do it quite a bit. I enjoy it and you'd be surprised how many people have never seen a handwritten letter. Besides, I think Father Dominic is a cool guy, and I believe he would appreciate it."

When Joe looked up, both Piper and Gabby were grinning at him.

"What?"

"Joe Chandler, you are a piece of work and I'm fortunate to know you."

"Ditto," said Piper.

"So," said Gabby, "that brings us to Señor Espinoza. What a change in fortunes! He was minutes away from giving us what we had come for, and then he gets his face shot off."

"Someone sure as hell didn't want him talking to us," said Piper. "You gotta figure those boys had been loyal to Espinoza for years."

"They knew he was only weeks from the grave, and so were their jobs."

"The way I see it," said Gabby, "that name cost the *señor* his life, but they sure as hell didn't figure on us. I just can't believe we were so close."

"I think it could have been worse," said Joe.

"Besides us getting killed," said Piper. "How could it have been worse?"

"Well, first of all, I was thinking about Señor Espinoza. How he'd escaped all the violence and resolved himself to dying of cancer. Then how he actually got a chance to, you know, sort of put his life in order and find some peace with his family and God."

Gabby and Piper stared at Joe.

"Sorry, guys, I didn't mean to get philosophical."

"No, that's actually right," said Gabby. "I was thinking of the same thing on the plane ride to Cozumel. He actually did get a second chance, and I think he took it."

"Yeah, maybe," said Piper. "But he still got his head blown off."

"Yes," said Joe. "He definitely lived by the sword and died by the sword, but still I think he got a chance to change his eternal destination. And when someone like Señor Espinoza finds grace, I don't know—it always makes me think how life can surprise you. However, what I was really getting at is that Señor Espinoza actually told us quite a bit."

"For instance?" asked Piper.

"Yeah," said Gabby. "For instance? All I can dwell on is the name we didn't get."

"All right, let's see. We learned that the cartels are worried about legalized pot, and . . . we know that we're looking for an American. He mentioned someone who knows people, someone with influence in

Washington DC, and he mentioned government contracts and making billions of dollars."

"That's a scary thought," said Gabby. "The idea that someone in our own nation's capital ordered the murder of seventeen little girls and just tried to kill the three of us."

"I agree," said Joe. "Espinoza was pretty clear we were dealing with people who had connections in Washington."

"Or worse," said Piper. "Maybe they are Washington. I've never trusted any of those power-hungry bottom-feeders."

"All right, boys: the director wants us at the office by 11:00 AM. We still have some flying to do and I still have a report to write. One thing you both can count on is that I will have your backs. Let's get some sleep and meet for coffee at 4:00 AM."

"4:00 AM!" said Piper. "Ah, man, I'm definitely going to miss the *relajado la vida de México.*"

CHAPTER 24

LUCILE

The M600 rolled onto the tarmac at Andrews Air Force Base at 8:20 AM, then taxied to a designated hangar where a suit and three USAF airmen were waiting. They secured the doors and unloaded the sensitive cargo into a waiting government van.

"Not sure where all that's headed," said Piper to the man in the suit, "but I've got some personal effects in there I've been toting around for years. I sure hope to see them again."

"No worries," said the suit. "You'll have your gear by tomorrow. I'll see to it personally. Grab your luggage and put it in the Suburban, I have orders to get you all cleaned up for a meeting at 1300 hours."

Joe caught the military time and, looking at the build of the man, figured he was probably ex-Special Forces.

"Listen, *amigo*," said Piper. "Any chance we could pull through a Starbucks? It's been awhile."

"Starbucks!" said the suit as he started the Suburban.

"Brother, you haven't had coffee until you've had a double shot café macchiato from Lucile's. Like me," said the suit, "Lucile is black, beautiful, and from Portland, Oregon. The sister can do things with an espresso machine and milk steamer that will rock your world. My name's Oscar," he said, flashing a big smile while sticking out his hand.

Piper grabbed it and turned to the backseat where Joe and Gabby were listening.

"I have a new best friend and his name is Oscar. Oscar, I'm Piper and you and I are going to get along just fine. Drive on, bro, and pray Lucile doesn't get a look at me or she'll never look your way again."

Oscar put on his shades, tilted his head back, and started singing.

> *"Lucile, you won't do your sister's will...*
> *Oh, Lucile, you won't do your sister's will...*
> *You ran off and married, but I love you still."*

Not missing a single beat, Piper laid back his head and belted out:

> *"Lucile, please come back where you belong,*
> *Lucile, please come back where you belong,*
> *I've been good to you, baby, please don't leave me alone."*

Gabby looked at Joe and rolled her eyes. "Oh, my God, it's the Blues Brothers. We're in the car with Jake and Elwood."

Oscar and Piper did a fist pump with a finger burst and sang the entire track of "Lucile" together.

After coffee and meeting the lovely Miss Lucile, they made a quick stop at Gabby's home in Falls Church, Virginia, where everyone freshened up and changed clothes.

As they all walked back to rejoin Oscar, who had waited out front, Piper whistled low and slow.

"Very nice digs here, Gabby; you have excellent taste."

"Thank you," she replied. "It was a mess when I bought it, but my dad, being somewhat of a craftsman, helped me restore it before I moved in. It was the eyesore of the street, so now I'm pretty popular with my neighbors."

As they climbed in and headed to the meeting, Joe looked at her and smiled.

"He's right, your home was beautiful and inviting —a rare combination. It's obvious your dad knew what he was doing. I love woodworking myself and was very impressed."

"Thank you. I love my dad and think of him every time I smell sawdust."

"Well, better than wine I guess."

"Ahhh, yeah, I would say so. What the heck does that even mean?"

"Oh, sorry, I grew up on a vineyard and I always equate the fragrance of wine and old oak barrels with my father."

Gabby furrowed her brow and glared back at him. "So, the wine in the restaurant, the bottle we had before we flew to Tucson, was that...."

"Yeah, sorry, I didn't want to sound snobbish."

"Good Lord, Chandler, will there ever be a day when you stop surprising me?"

"Does it come as a surprise that I'm a little nervous about this meeting? For some reason, it feels more like an exit interview."

"Look, Joe, we lost our source right in the same room as us; then we were arrested carrying weapons in a foreign country. Piper and I may be out of a job and you might well be court-martialed. What are you worried about?"

Without turning around, Piper said, "I heard that. Losing your job is overrated, Joe. I've done it several times and look at me—no worries."

"Oh, great!" said Oscar. "I thought ya'll were heroes or something. There better not be any collateral damage or guilt by association. Look, man, I just got this job."

"We'll be fine, everybody relax. As far as I'm concerned, I am in the company of heroes."

"Well, one for sure," mumbled Oscar.

They pulled to the front of the building where four MPs were waiting.

"Boy, that don't look good. Listen, good meeting ya'll and good luck and everything, but please don't mention my name when we stop."

"So much for new best friends," said Piper as he climbed out.

"Ms. Mendez?" asked one of the military policemen.

"That would be me."

"Welcome home, ma'am. If you would please follow me, I'll see you to your meeting."

Another MP asked for Mr. Longmire and, after verifying his ID, asked Piper to follow him. And it was the same for Joe, except he was escorted by the two remaining men. All three—Gabby, Piper, and Joe—were taken into the building then immediately separated.

So, it's going to be like this, thought Gabby. *They want three accounts of the incident and see if the stories conflict or mesh.*

When it became clear, each account of Mexico was relatively identical; the three were reunited in a large conference room where there was a table of sandwiches, fruit, and chips. Finally, at 1:00 PM, they were ushered into the director's office where Ralph Valenzuela and Lt. Col. Pike were already seated.

"I'm very sorry about the welcome home you received this morning, but it is protocol and everyone wants to cover their asses. We had to write the Mexican government a pretty fat check that caused some hubbub over at State, but they'll get over it. First, let me say that I'm thrilled everyone's all right and safely back on American soil. It looks like you walked into a nasty situation down there and, everything considered, it could have been a whole lot worse. The colonel will fill you in, then I'd like to get back on top of this as soon as possible. Sergeant, it was a pleasure working with you and if the opportunity arises, I'll be in touch." The director stood, shook their hands, and exited the room.

"Excuse me, Colonel," asked Joe, "but it sounded as if the director was excusing me from the mission?"

"You would be correct in that assumption, Sergeant Chandler, and I was just about to address that. As you can imagine, the Agency has taken some heat for stealing an active-duty Ranger, but since your MOS was intelligence, we fudged a little. However, as unfortunate as it is for us, I'm afraid our justification has run out, and to be determined by your superiors at the RSTB, you will be reassigned.

"Gabby, you of course will continue to work this case here at Langley.

And Longmire, until further notice, you will remain on this mission as well. I'm afraid we have to break up a good team, but such is the nature of our business.

"I would like to add the obvious: we all hoped this would end with either the capture or elimination of Juan Espinoza, but instead he's laid it right back on our doorstep. However, we are grateful for the work you did in Mexico, and we'll just have to keep doing our jobs. I will excuse myself and give you folks a few moments together. Gabby, as I understand it, your presence is required in the situation room. Thank you all and it was a pleasure working with you."

After Lt. Col. Pike left the room, the three stared out the window.

"Wow, just like it," said Piper. "Sometimes I hate this stinking job. However, it was a pleasure, and Joe, I wouldn't be surprised to see your smiling face again. You are a rare character, Mr. Chandler, and I shall look forward to our next visit."

Piper, knowing he was a third wheel, shook Joe's hand and walked out.

"Well, holy guacamole," said Gabby. She and Joe enjoyed a good laugh at Piper's expense, but they had both come to love and respect him immensely.

"Listen, Gabby, I… well, I just wanted to say…."

"Yeah, me too, Joe, but remember I work for an intelligence agency, so don't try to hide."

Joe smiled at her; they hugged and walked out the door in opposite directions.

"Hey, Joe…."

He stopped and turned.

"Don't forget to pray for me, okay?"

Joe smiled, nodded, and walked away.

CHAPTER 25

Romeo

The following morning with coffee in hand, as Mel walked toward her office, she was intercepted by Sarah, her admin.

"Just a heads-up, boss: there's a man waiting for you, and he's very adamant that you see him."

"Any idea who he is or what this is about?"

"None whatsoever, but he says it has to do with Mr. Crivelli. Oh, and he's Hispanic and really cute."

"Oh, well, as long as he's cute," snipped Mel.

The man was seated in a small waiting room and stood when Mel approached. He was wearing an expensive suit and carrying a worn black leather briefcase. Mel introduced herself and asked how she could be of help.

"Ms. Randle, my name is Romeo Banderas and, if you have a few minutes, I would like to speak with you regarding a matter of concern to both of us."

Well, of course, your name is Romeo, thought Mel. "I'm afraid I have a very busy day, Mr. Banderas, but I can spare a few minutes. Why don't you come into my office? Would you like some tea or coffee... water perhaps?"

"No, thank you, I'm fine. But if you don't mind, it's a delicate matter and I wonder if you'd mind closing the door?"

Mel stared at the man from across her desk, opened a drawer where she kept a CZ 9-mm pistol that Joe had given her, then pressed the intercom asking her admin to come into her office.

When Sarah walked in, Mel said, "Sarah, this is Mr. Banderas. He was about to show you some identification."

Romeo smiled, pulled his wallet from his briefcase, pulled out a business card and ID, and handed both to Sarah who read them out loud.

"Yes, it appears that Mr. Roman Banderas lives in Guadalajara, Mexico, and is a senior partner for the firm of Banderas, Colon, and Munoz." She handed the ID back to Mr. Banderas and the card to Mel. "Is there anything else, boss?"

"That will be all, Sarah; please close the door on your way out and tell the sheriff I will be with him shortly."

Romeo smiled. "I admire a wise and cautious woman, Ms. Randle; well done."

"Thank you, Mr. Banderas; now what is this all about, exactly?"

"Ms. Randle: some time ago, a good friend of yours did a great service for a client of mine, and now he wishes to return the favor. My client was quite impressed with the character and wisdom of your friend and now considers him his friend as well. You see, Ms. Randle, my firm represents the Holy Roman Catholic Church in Mexico and my client's name is Archbishop Dominic Antonio Gonzalez Iglesias. Your friend would remember him as Father Gonzalez."

"Yes, Mr. Banderas, I have heard my friend speak very fondly of the monsignor, but isn't this a conversation you should be having with my friend?"

"That is an excellent point, Ms. Randle; however, once I explain, I believe you will understand why I have come to you first."

CHAPTER 26

GABBY

For the past forty-two months of his enlistment, Sergeant Joseph Chandler had served his country with distinction. Given his choice of any duty station he preferred, he was assigned to the Defense Language Institute in Monterey, California. He co-taught common Arabic and lectured at a community college when invited. On a foggy November morning, forty-five days before his discharge from the Army, he answered his cell phone and recognized a familiar voice.

"Got time to buy an old friend a cup of coffee?"

Joe met Piper at an espresso bar on Lighthouse Avenue. They exchanged a few pleasantries but Joe could see the weight on Piper's shoulders.

"What brings you to the West Coast, Piper?"

"Joe, it's Gabby. She was shot and killed three nights ago. It hasn't hit the wires yet and I didn't want you to hear about it on CNN."

The three of them had stayed in touch by email or the occasional phone call. The previous Christmas, Joe and Gabby had agreed to meet at his parents, but duty called and she'd been forced to cancel at the last minute. She apologized and told Joe she'd come see him right after she chased down some promising leads.

The color went out of his face and his eyes clouded with tears. Nothing was said for several moments as Joe tried to find his voice.

"How, when, and where, Piper?"

"Look, Joe, I don't need to tell you how restricted this damn case is. Seriously, bro, this thing is buttoned-up tight. The only reason I know about Gabby is because I flew her up to Oregon once and, technically, I was still part of the mission."

"Oregon? I didn't know the case was taking her to the northwest. Come on, Piper, I have the same clearance you do."

"Okay, pal, but you didn't hear it from me. Apparently, she figured something out—something big and it had to do with someone from Oregon. She was presenting her report to the director the following morning when someone shot her in her driveway. She'd just driven home from the airport and it was late and ... well, they were waiting for her. Of course they took her briefcase, phone, and laptop. A neighbor saw the interior light of her car and came over and found her. I'm very sorry, Joe. I know how fond of her you were."

"It was someone she knew," said Joe.

"What do you mean, pal?"

"Gabby was nervous; she told me she felt like she was being followed and was worried about who she could trust. She used the term 'billions' and said this thing was bigger than anyone could imagine, and promised me that she was being careful. It had to have been someone she knew. There is no way anyone else would have gotten the drop on her. She was too good, Piper; she was too dang good."

The funeral was at Arlington National Cemetery and was well attended. Joe stood next to Piper and Colonel Pike. Because of the tremendous backlog at Arlington, Gabby's funeral was a week after Joe's discharge. In an age of the forty-eight-hour news cycle, two months was enough time for some to forget, and the rest were just too damn busy. On the other hand Joe would never forget, nor would he forget those who were responsible.

He went home to Segundo Vida Vineyards, where he grieved the death of his dear friend. His parents, whom he had seen on the occasional holiday, embraced him and showed him immeasurable grace. It was only weeks after New Year's, the vineyard was dormant and there was little for him to do. Joe came to an agreement with his father: he would spend a day or two each week at the vineyard, but he wanted to open an espresso bar and bakery. Gabby's death was eating away at him, and he needed something to do to channel his anger and keep him sane. Drummer and Lizzie gave him their blessings. Occasionally, however, Joe would leave to "buy coffee." He had made a promise to find those responsible for his friend's murder.

CHAPTER 27

PROVIDENCE

Mel read the letter again, and a cold chill ran down her spine. "This is not possible; it just can't be. Oh my God, it just can't be."

Romeo Banderas watched Mel's hands tremble as she read the letter a third time.

"I understand your grave concern, Ms. Randle, but perhaps now would be a good time to invite Mr. Chandler to our meeting, do you not agree?"

Joe read the letter from his good friend, Father Dominic, now the Archbishop of Guadalajara, for a second time.

Joseph, my dear son, I miss our talks and it is my prayer that you are able to come to visit me one day soon. I would like to say more on this matter, but there is some disturbing information that has ***providentially*** *found its way to me. I asked God to forgive me for breaking the confidence of a repentant soul.*

There is a wealthy and powerful man in my diocese, one who makes generous donations to help the poor. This man requested an audience, which I granted, and he made an unusual request. He asked if I could, "wash away the filth of the Americans."

I told him God was merciful, but I must admit that I was curious, much too curious for a confessor.

It is Mexico, my son, and it is not uncommon for a priest to hear the confessions of such men, so I told him to bare his soul and tell me everything.

The man explained that he had a business arrangement with a group of powerful Americans—dangerous men who were not afraid to "dispose" of people who got in their way.

It was difficult for him but he spoke of a recent meeting in California. He was asked to ***"encourage"*** *certain farmers in Mexico to stop raising their prices. He said he would encourage them and they would listen.*

Then, one of the Americans suggested that a ***"second obstacle"*** *needed to be removed. When I asked which American he looked at me, knowing that it was a question I should not ask. I simply shrugged my shoulders and a moment later he said it was her teacher, the one from the university in Palo Alto. This professor wrote down a woman's name, a young district attorney from Oregon. When I asked what he knew about the first obstacle, he was very defensive. He said he had nothing to do with the woman in Virginia; it had been the gringo. When I asked about this gringo, he crossed himself and said he was the angel of death, and a man he feared. He did not mention any names or elaborate further.*

The news of Señorita Mendez's death was late coming to my ears, but I grieved and prayed for her soul. I prayed for you as well, knowing how fond of her you were.

It was Romeo who looked into this matter and discovered the name of Ms. Randle—a recent Stanford graduate working as a district attorney in Oregon. I would not think it a difficult task for her to discover the professor's name.

I believed you would find this information helpful, as I know you to be a man who still does God's work. You remain dear to my heart and I remain your servant.

Father Dominic

"So, there is no doubt about the information then?"

"Señor Chandler, you of all people know how careful the archbishop is in these matters. It is why there was no phone call, no email, or use of your postal system. It is a very grave matter, señor, and it is why I am here."

"Oh my God, Joe, I called Professor Trudeau a few weeks ago. I told him about my suspicions and he seemed very eager to help me, and he insisted I keep him updated. He even told me to be careful whom I confided in, and to bounce everything off of him first. I called him again last week, and when he asked if I had any names, I mentioned Bill Crivelli and possible associates of his. Oh my God, Joe, what have I done?"

Joe and Romeo finally got Mel calmed down and explained how fortunate they were to have this information.

"Look, Mel, this is the big leagues, maybe as big as it gets, and I don't blame you for being scared."

"Scared, I'm not scared, Joe—I'm pissed. Someone who was once very dear to me just ordered my execution. And right now, it seems likely that he and his associates may have had your friend killed as well."

"Mr. Banderas," said Joe. "I cannot thank you and Father Dominic enough. I would say it was providential indeed, and now we must get busy to exploit this information. Fortunately, I have a few powerful friends as well."

CHAPTER 28

Dr. John

While Dr. John Grossman may have disgraced himself as a congressman and slipped out of town in the middle of the night, he landed on his feet. As a respected medical doctor and unabashed liberal, he won a seat in the House, representing the sixth congressional district of Oregon. He had beaten out a brilliant conservative economist by painting him as a gun-toting, bigoted Christian who hated gays, trees, and the environment. One such ad denounced him as a racist, but seeing that he and his Asian wife had adopted four African children the spot was pulled, but the damage was done—Dr. John had shamelessly stolen the moral high ground and was swept into office.

He served four terms and made a name for himself as a proponent of euthanasia or, as he called it, "peaceful pass." During his second term, he coauthored an unsuccessful bill for the nationwide legalization of medical marijuana. Then, redeeming himself, Dr. John very quietly orchestrated a referendum that quickly thwarted an effort by conservative Republicans to end the exemption of House members from the questionable services of the Affordable Care Act, or Obama Care, for which he received the accolades of members from both sides of the aisle.

Dr. John was a rising star inside the beltway and, as politicians often do, he began to feel untouchable. Since he was a medical doctor, and it was health care, Dr. John used his influence in procuring funds for the Oregon State Health Care Exchange. Working with his friends back home and being cheered on by the governor, Dr. John secured over three hundred million dollars in a federal grant to establish the Oregon State Exchange. As a reward, his longtime live-in friend was hired to oversee the establishment and implementation of the enrollment website. Strangely, a year later, not a single person was able to use the website, and the entire program was scrapped in lieu of the federal exchange.

The real problems for Dr. John and his "friend" escalated once a picture surfaced of the two walking hand in hand next to a million-dollar condo in Laguna Beach, or, perhaps, it was the new Mercedes convertible that pushed things over the edge; nevertheless, over the edge they did go. Forced to resign in lieu of impeachment, Dr. John Grossman, *his friend*, and about one hundred million dollars disappeared from Oregon, only to resurface two years later in a posh neighborhood of Arlington, Virginia. While Dr. John may never again hold public office, the scandal had not affected his sense of smell. And as the winds of change were blowing, he and his longtime lover smelled opportunity.

CHAPTER 29

LOUIE TRUDEAU

It all began thirteen years earlier when Dr. John and his friend, René, were walking through the French village of Saint-Tropez. They were sitting at a sidewalk café enjoying a cappuccino when a familiar face happened by.

"Louie Trudeau, is that you?"

Louie almost didn't turn around, but seeing René out the corner of his eye, he slowed and then stopped. He looked a bit paranoid, but was happy to see an old adversary. When Louie had been burning up the courtrooms of LA as a prosecutor, he had run into this whip-smart defense attorney on more than one occasion. For those who could afford them, the firm of Madison, Grey, and Dumont were not whom prosecutors wanted to see across the aisle of a courtroom.

"René Dumont—my goodness, it has been awhile!"

Both René and John stood as introductions were made.

"For Christ's sake, Louie, please sit down and do tell me everything. You just dropped off the face of the earth and left us all wondering if you were wearing cement shoes in the Catalina Straights. I missed you, Louie, you were the only real talent the DA's office could muster. If I recall, I believe you bested me more than once."

"I must say it has been a while since I've seen or spoken to anyone from LA, but unfortunately it's how it had to be. I was so tired, René. When I came home late one night and found my Golden Retriever hanging from a tree in my backyard, I just packed and left town. Like you said I was about to be fitted for cement shoes, and that last case may have actually done me in."

"That was Carmelo Rossi the casino guy, right?"

"Yeah, that's him. I couldn't get anyone to testify on the pedophile charges, but we did put him away for five-to-ten on a racketeering and tax evasion conviction. However, it was the headlines in the *Times* regarding the pedophile charges that probably sealed my fate. I think that Sicilian bastard is still looking for me."

"Well, Louie, if you're going to hide you sure picked a nice place, and I swear your secret is safe with us."

After moving down the street to a club and switching from coffee to wine, the conversation shifted to Dr. John.

"He's not convinced yet, Louie, but this bright orthopedic surgeon is about to be Oregon's newest legislator."

"I wish you both well, and if I lived in Oregon I'd come back just to vote for you."

"You can't stay away forever, Louie; why don't you come home?"

"There is nothing I'd like more. Actually, I just finished my PhD in criminal law and thought about doing some teaching."

CHAPTER 30

LOBBYING 101

A year after the chance meeting in Saint-Tropez, René Dumont contacted Louie Trudeau, JD-PhD, and told him to come home. The first bit of news was that Carmelo Luigi Rossi had been shot and killed by the father of a molestation victim. The deciding factor, that made Louie go to his rented townhouse and pack, was an interview arranged by René at Stanford University. Apparently, they were in the market for a new criminal law professor, and René knew a friend of a friend.

America runs on a forty-eight-hour news cycle and, after a year, the entire country has amnesia. The lists of gross negligence and the outright criminal accusations associated with the Affordable Care Act reached deep and wide. Some had forgotten his name, and even fewer remembered the sins of Dr. John Grossman. If anything, he was a member of a large fraternity who had capitalized on a behemoth federal program with little or no oversight.

Before a single state had outright legalized cannabis, the decriminalization process was well on its way. By the end of the seventies, a dozen states had decriminalized the possession of marijuana, and a dozen more quit prosecuting anyone who wasn't selling. In 1996, the first medical marijuana dispensary opened in Fairfax, California. Several states had decriminalized it, then recriminalized, so to some degree—it was still a wait-and-see game. However, for Dr. John Grossman and René Dumont, the waiting was over. They had started a lobbying group for the legalization of medical marijuana in all fifty states. Dr. John had spoken at every venue imaginable—from radical potheads at Berkley, AMA conventions in Orlando, to a senate subcommittee on the Hill.

Representing the tens of thousands of patients who benefitted from various forms of cannabis was, in the minds of many, an honorable endeavor. However, Dr. John and René were substantially more ambitious than a petty, not-for-profit lobbying group. While the missing money from the federal coffers, earmarked for Oregon's Health Care Exchange, was all but forgotten, it was now being put to good use as seed money for building coalitions, friendships, support, and protection. The two men had decided years earlier exactly where they were headed, and both realized the billions of dollars at stake for controlling America's *legal* marijuana trade. René had been extremely cautious and, using a tax shelter attorney from the Cayman Islands, had buried their endeavors and their identities deep inside an offshore cooperation called *North of Here, Inc.*

CHAPTER 31

ARCHIE

Mel spent Thanksgiving with her family in California and Christmas in Oregon, among her best friends. The vineyard was aglow with strings of lights and decorated trees inside and out. On Christmas Eve, Jose pulled a large hay wagon as family and friends drank eggnog and sang Christmas carols. They did the loop through the valley, finally stopping for a midnight worship service at a small country church.

The party at Hobie and Jillian's was the best New Year's celebration she could ever remember. It was all a fairytale until Romeo Banderas had brought the letter.

Joe and Mel went to the vineyard where they were able to work and think in a secure environment. They pieced together everything they had, drawing circles, adding brackets, and putting it all on paper. After the final edit and agreeing on their course of action, they asked for a meeting with Drummer, the mayor, and Archie Anderson.

Mel began by asking everyone to bear with them.

"Archie, Joe told me you lost a son several years ago—an automobile accident I believe."

Archie looked puzzled as to why Mel wanted to scrape the scab off a very painful wound.

"That's correct. He was the driver of the car and hit a lumber train at a crossing out in the country. While it was a very dark, rainy night, it was determined that he and the three passengers were all high on marijuana and, unfortunately, no one survived."

"And you've been a fierce opponent of the legalization of marijuana ever since."

"Mel, with every fiber of my being I believed the legalization of recreational marijuana will do more harm than good. However, now that it is the law, all I can do is to try and slow its destructive grip on the children of this country."

"And Mayor Abercrombe, you support your friend in his efforts, isn't that correct?"

"That's correct, Mel. It's getting damn hard to fight the tide of drugs but, like Archie, I do what I can."

It was Joe's turn to connect a few dots.

"Look, everyone: Mel and I have some information which probably links Bill Crivelli to the marijuana industry. We don't have concrete evidence as of yet, but I have some friends back in Washington and Virginia who may be able to help with that. Archie, we believe it is your outspoken stance against marijuana, not to mention being the DA, which has made you a target of Bill Crivelli and his very dangerous partners. I've never talked much about my time in the military, but I wasn't just fighting terrorism. I spent a great deal of time investigating the murderous cartels that are flooding our country with illegal drugs. We are talking about billions of dollars in profits, and, right now, I believe we are dealing with people who want to use our land and resources to grow marijuana. Our soil is perfect and we have a seemingly endless supply of water. It is my suspicion there may be 'Bill Crivellis' in other promising agriculture regions of the country. Furthermore, I think they are all working on behalf of a co-op, if you will, with powerful allies in Washington DC. I believe they are trying to buy land, corner the market, and get rid of the opposition; and, furthermore, I believe these may be the people responsible for killing my friend, Gabby. Mel and I are leaving for a few days, so keep your eyes open and, please, say nothing."

CHAPTER 32

The Team

For over an hour, Joe Chandler got the run-around from operators, various sergeants, and eventually he was transferred to security. However, Joe wasn't looking for security—he was trying to get a call through to Lt. Col. Pike but instead was getting the ole agency two-step by people who didn't know him from Adam. Joe finally gave up, telling Mel it was easier to get through to the complaint department of a cable TV company. He hit a contact number on his cell phone and, within seconds, had a real person on the line.

"Holy guacamole, I was just thinking of you. What's up, brother?"

"Piper, I wish I had time to visit but I need to get in contact with Pike and I've been jerked around by NSA for an hour. Any chance you could have him call me? It's pretty important."

"I guess you haven't heard then. When we lost Gabby, someone on the Hill, someone with some serious machismo, started digging into our investigation. The next thing you know, we're over budget and somebody is accusing everybody of incompetence. Director Valenzuela got involved, but even he didn't have the chutzpah to save the mission or Col. Pike. As of last week, the mission is officially shut down and Pike, who was a shoo-in for full bird, got passed over for promotion. As you know, that was a death knell to his career. Right now he's rotting in a back office over at the Pentagon, and no one seems to know why."

"I sure would like to find out who wanted that file closed. Piper, where exactly are you?"

"At the moment I'm trying to be invisible. I have an office here at Langley that looks more like a utility room with an ironing board as a desk."

"Piper, our flight into Dulles lands at 10:00 PM. We're staying at the Hilton over at Tyson's Corner. Any chance you and Pike could meet us for an early breakfast?"

"I can't foresee it being a problem, but I'll text you a confirmation. I have a pretty good idea that both Pike and I could shoot pool all day and no one would miss us. It'll be good to see you, Joe, have a safe flight."

At 6:30 AM, Pike and Piper walked into the Founding Farmers Restaurant off the 495 Freeway. Both taking no chances, wore jeans and ball caps.

"Thanks for coming; it's good to see you both. This is Mel Randle, my very good friend and the assistant district attorney from my hometown in Oregon."

Both men smiled, said hello to Mel, then Pike looked at Joe.

"First of all, Joe, if this is about the mission, you are no longer privy to classified material and we both could be arrested for thinking about it, much less talking to you. Secondly, I do not know Ms. Randle, and last but certainly not least, I am assuming this must be damn important or I wouldn't be here. However, Joe, if you want me to risk a firing squad, this better be really good."

Joe looked at Mel who nodded for him to continue.

"We believe the same people who killed Gabby also ordered a hit on Mel. That means there is a connection, right? Furthermore, I think they may have deep enough pockets and good enough connections to have someone torpedo your career. Do I have your attention yet?"

"Joe, I would say you have my undivided attention; please continue."

"We don't want to get you or anyone into trouble, Colonel, no worse than you already are. It seems obvious someone is going out of their way to shut down a viable mission—one with confirmed intel and good open leads. And, Colonel, to do so, they are willing to kill Gabby and throw your career under the bus. We need help—someone with creds and clearance and, right now, I assume you still have both."

Joe explained how they had begun examining the practices and intentions of a man named Bill Crivelli, mostly as an effort to protect some good friends. Then both Joe and Mel laid out their hypothesis that some extremely dangerous men with powerful connections in the US government were trying to corner the market and distribution channels of medical and recreational marijuana. Next, Joe handed each of them a copy of the letter from Father Dominic. They both had to read it twice.

"You must be kidding," said Piper. "What is the chance of that happening, Joe? I mean, it's almost spooky, right?"

"So, let me get this straight," said Pike, looking at Mel. "A priest in Guadalajara, who is a good friend to Joe, takes a confession from a man who probably runs a team of Mexican thugs and hitmen, who just happens to have been asked by one of your ex-law professors, whom he has a business relationship with, to kill *you*, Ms. Randle. Is that correct?"

"That is correct, Colonel. The monsignor and Joe referred to it as providence, and I do not have a better explanation—do you, sir?"

"Well, I certainly hope you both bought a Powerball ticket at the airport, and Piper's correct: it's downright spooky. Do you have any idea who this 'gringo' might be?"

Joe told them he didn't have that piece of the puzzle.

"You are right, Joe, it is a puzzle and perhaps I may be able to add a few missing piece."

"Now, you have *my* full attention, Colonel."

"Right before they pulled the plug on our investigation, we caught a series of breaks—breaks that should have expedited the case instead of shutting it down.

"First of all, if you remember, we were squeezing Tino Alvarez who finally gave us something. Tino told an FBI agent named Irwin that a 'badass gringo soldier' gave him some serious cash to betray Espinoza, and then hooked him up with Javier Rivera. As it turns out, one of our agents down in Tijuana was running an informant named Castro, who worked for Rivera. Astonishingly, the kid was able to snap a picture of an American. He told Agent Castro that Rivera was scared to death of this guy, and said he looked like a soldier. I have the photo but it's blurred, and before I could get it run through the system we were out of business.

"Another promising break came from a wiretap of an ex-midlevel FDA employee by the name of Lonnie Rudman. We listened to a conversation between Rudman and a lowlife hacker known as Luther. The gist of the conversation certainly validates your hypothesis about someone wanting to take Mexico out of the equation and control the legal pot industry.

Eventually we heard a second conversation, and we got a name. We think Rudman was getting cold feet and made a phone call to his boss. When he or she answered, Rudman said, 'Listen, René,' and the person on the other end said, 'If you ever use my name on the phone or call me at this number again, I'll have someone cut your sack off,' and the line went dead."

"Why do you say he or she?" asked Mel.

"Because we naturally assumed the name René was a woman, but the voice, no matter how many times we analyzed it, could have gone either way."

"My God," said Mel. "As a prosecutor I would stand up and cheer with this kind of evidence. Granted it's not enough to take to trial, but it certainly does not warrant shutting down an investigation; actually, quite the opposite."

"My thoughts exactly," said Pike.

The four were quiet as the waitress refilled their coffee cups and laid down the check, and they remained quiet for several moments longer.

"Whew, that's a lot to take in, but definitely too much to sit on," said Pike, obviously deep in thought. "I still have my clearance and a computer, but what I really need is someone at Langley. All the case files are encrypted and I no longer have access."

"I agree," said Joe.

"We need to connect this whole thing to one person, or one identifiable group. Someone is in charge and that someone is behind Gabby's murder, and I will not quit until I find them."

"All right, boys," said Mel. "Let's look at what we got. We know Professor Trudeau is in this thing up to his neck, but I doubt he's the guy—agreed?"

Everyone nodded and Joe responded. "I agree that he's up to his neck, but I think Mel's right: I think we're looking for someone who's a lot more connected on the Hill; if not a sitting politician, then probably a staffer or a lobbyist or some such. We definitely have to shake down Trudeau, but not at the risk of giving away our position."

Again, everyone nodded and Mel continued. "That leaves us with Bill Crivelli, a corporation named North of Here, Inc., Lonnie Rudman, a mysterious soldier, a photo of a possible American soldier in Mexico, and a man or woman named René. So, who takes what and how do we proceed?"

They planned, plotted, divided responsibilities, and agreed to meet the following evening for dinner.

CHAPTER 33

RENÉ

Lindsey climbed into the cab with René, and they both climbed out at Twigs, in the lobby of the Capital Hilton. The lunch fare was always good and it was more discreet than Café Milano or Charlie Palmers.

"I wanted to thank you, Lindsey, and show my appreciation. I owe you one."

Lindsey was a senior staffer for a New York senator, one with oversight responsibilities for the CIA. While the CIA inevitably reports to the president, and Congress can exercise some authority over its purse strings, the Senate Intelligence Oversight Committee is about as close to accountability as the CIA ever encounters. It just so happened Lindsey worked for a senator on that same committee and Lindsey was crazy about René and would do anything to get his attention.

"Actually, René, it wasn't that difficult. That investigation was dragging on with little to show for it and, as it turned out, my boss and Director Raphael Valenzuela have butted heads on more than one occasion. It was terribly unfortunate about all those poor dears from Nicaragua but sometimes it *is* best to move on, don't you think, René?"

What René thought was how incredibly stupid and gullible Lindsey was.

"Actually, kitten, I think they were from Guatemala, but yes sometimes it's best to move on. By the way, any word from the other side of the aisle regarding the new medical marijuana research exemption bill?"

Dr. John had been extremely busy knocking doors on Capitol Hill. He had paid especially close attention to the representatives from "good-ole-boy" states. He knew their greatest obstacles would come from the very red Bible belt. Both he and René also knew that playing the compassion card for the sick and suffering was their best chance to remove another nail from the door obstructing legalization in all fifty states.

"I think we may have picked up one more vote from West Virginia. Those poor folks over there are dropping like flies from lung cancer. Dr. John may have convinced the senator that federal-funded cannabis oil would be an affordable option for the struggling folks of his state."

"That's good to hear, Lindsey. We . . . I appreciate it very much."

"I'm glad to know I've made you happy, René; maybe one day soon we can still take that cruise."

"Of course, kitten."

CHAPTER 34

THE PLAN

Piper had rented a month-to-month flat on the south end of Georgetown. It was a duplex, and since the place next door was empty, it became their base of operation. The colonel's wife, Demi Pike, was used to her husband's work as well as the absences, and was always happy to pitch in. In this case, she made a large platter of triple chocolate brownies, sent them with her husband, and told him she wouldn't wait up.

The draft was good but it needed a few tweaks and the team would need a few breaks. After pizza, they rolled up their sleeves and ironed out the details.

"I told Demi," began Pike, "if I'm being thrown over after nineteen years of stellar service, I was going out with a bang. She told me to make it a loud one, and just so everyone knows, I'm all in."

"I guess this one's off the record then," said Piper. "Because at this juncture, I'm not sure who we can trust."

All eyes shifted to Joe.

"Thanks, everyone. I believe we have a good plan and depending on how it goes in the next twenty-four hours, we'll regroup and start phase two. Remember, they think Mel incidentally stumbled onto

Crivelli, and they have no idea we've joined forces. We should have the upper hand.

"Everyone knows their role, but let's go over it all again to make sure we're not missing anything. With God's help and the right bait, maybe we'll land the big fish."

CHAPTER 35

The Bait

There were several unanswered questions, but a big one was who would Bill Crivelli call if he got nervous. One of Mel's responsibilities was to find out. Taking into consideration the time difference back in Oregon, Mel waited until she was certain Katie Sandburg was in her office.

"Good morning, Ms. Sandburg! How are you this fine day?"

"My goodness, don't you sound chipper, Ms. Randle. What exactly may I do for you?"

"Actually, Katie, I'm in DC and I'm a day or two away from asking the FBI to open an investigation into the business practices of Bill Crivelli and his known associates."

"You can't be serious, Mel; you're actually in DC, as in Washington DC, and you did say FBI, right?"

"I am, I did, and I'm afraid I'm in a bit of a hurry, so if you would be a darling, I need you to pull up some land purchase records for me. I could go through the courthouse but I'm trying to keep this confidential, and I figured, as one attorney to another, you were my safest bet. So, pull anything in the last five years with either Crivelli's name or a corporation called North of Here, Inc. Did you get that?"

"Yeah, I got it, I wrote it down."

"It would be a great favor, Katie, and remember, please keep this quiet. I believe you know my admin, Sarah, so give her a buzz when you have them and she'll stop by and pick everything up. Okay, Katie, I gotta run, but I do owe you one."

Mel hung up, called her office, and Sarah answered. She told her to expect a call from Katie and explained how to handle it. Sarah couldn't stand the city attorney and welcomed the opportunity to play along.

The pretty lieutenant who left her cell number on Joe's arm had a name, and now it was Lieutenant Commander Alexandra Coleman.

"Hi, this is Alex. If you're not afraid, leave your number and I'll consider calling you back."

Joe laughed and thought what a perfect recording for the "pretty lieutenant" and the only message he left was his name. In thirty seconds, his cell rang.

"Well, well, well, who said prayers aren't answered. Joseph Chandler, please tell me you're not married with three children."

"Hello, Alex. I see you haven't changed."

She laughed out loud. "Are you in town?"

"Alex, I need a favor; it's a big one . . . and it's for Gabby."

"I see. Well, damn, what am I supposed to say to that? I can meet you at Greenberry's Coffee on Redmond Drive. How about 11:30?"

"You're a sweetheart, Alex. Thank you."

"Don't say it if you don't mean it, Joe. And besides, maybe you're fat and bald now and I won't mind saying no to you."

"Eleven thirty then."

A phone on a desk inside a small office at the Central Intelligence Agency rang, and a strong, confident voice said, "Agent Briggs."

"Lucile, please come back where you belong,
I've been good to you baby, please don't leave me alone."

"That is one fine song, Piper, and you may be the only white man I know who can give it the swag it deserves. What do I owe the pleasure, my very good friend?"

"First of all, I need one of those double shot café macchiato from Lucile's."

"Oh, boy, here it comes. Why do I feel like I need to hang up on your sorry ass right now?"

"It's for Gabby, bro."

"I'm off at 1500 hours, I'll meet you there."

Almost no one paid attention to the lieutenant colonel who was simply bidding his time before being nudged out the door. Occasionally a menial task was required, but the word was the once hotshot mission leader was poison, so keep your distance. That was perfectly fine with Lt. Col. Pike who was happy to be ignored, so he could do his own bidding. For the last several hours he had researched and pored through file after file, looking for a connection between Lonnie Rudman and someone with much larger *cojones.* As close as he'd gotten was an employer disclosure request sent to Mr. Rudman from the IRS. Chasing the lead into the following year, he struck gold when he found a copy of the reply. The stated employer was an international business corporation—North of Here, Inc.

CHAPTER 36

THE VIRTUOUS WOMAN

The espresso cafe was half-filled and Lt. Commander Alexandra Coleman was waiting at a back table with two coffees.

"My goodness, Joe, so much for fat and bald; I see civilian life is treating you *very* well. You are still looking your same amazing self."

"Hello, Alex. You haven't changed one bit. Still the most beautiful girl at the Agency I suppose?"

"Well, I certainly think so; however, there is a new Marine JAG officer who was Miss Something-or-the-Other of the Month. She's turning a few heads, but I'm not worried.

"Okay, Joe, enough of your shallow compliments; I know when I'm being rejected, which usually doesn't happen, all right? But regardless, what kind of a favor?"

"Alex, I'm going to give you a list of names and I desperately need to know how they're connected."

Joe slipped the paper across the table.

"Recognize anyone?"

"Sure; I remember seeing Lonnie Rudman's name from a FISA request I filled out, but look, this is some serious stuff, Joe. They shut this thing down quickly, and everything to do with that investigation was sealed 'CONFIDENTIAL,' and all interested parties were told, rather abruptly I might add, to butt out."

"I understand, Alex, but one of these people either killed Gabby or they work for whoever did."

Alex looked at the list one more time. "Is René a man or woman?"

"I'd really like to know the answer to that, Alex. Please see what you can find and, if it gets weird, bail out and there will be no hard feeling from me."

Alex raised her eyebrows and exhaled long and slow. "If this was any weirder, Joe, it would be a new episode of *The X-Files*. Let me see what I can do. Gabby and I didn't always see eye to eye, but she damn sure didn't deserve what happened."

Joe grabbed her arm and, with an ink pen, wrote something on her wrist. When he stood he leaned over and kissed her cheek, then turned and walked away.

She watched him then yelled, "That drink's still on me!"

Without turning around he raised his hand and walked through the door. She looked at her wrist again. Joe had written *Prov. 31:10*. She furrowed her brow, grabbed her iPhone, Googled "Prov. 31:10," and found it was a quote from the Old Testament of the Bible:

> ***"Who can find a virtuous woman? For her price is far above rubies."***

Her eyes misted ever so slightly and she whispered, "*Damn you, Joseph Chandler.*"

Piper and Agent Oscar Briggs ordered coffee at Lucile's Espresso. Piper skipped the names and a few details but brought Oscar up to speed and the possibility of what may be coming down.

"Sometimes these things take an unexpected twist and we would really appreciate the backup, Oscar."

"Piper, I knew you were going to eventually get my ass fired or killed."

"Hey, I get it, pal; if you can't do it, I completely understand."

"Homie, I wouldn't miss it for the world. Besides, I could always marry Lucile and learn to make a mean macchiato—count me in."

By the time Joe got back to Piper's townhouse, Mel was pretty animated. Her face was buried in her laptop and she was burning up the keyboard.

"What's going on, partner? You look like a cat about to pounce on a cornered mouse."

"Pike called about an hour ago, and guess where Lonnie Rudman gets his paycheck? *North of Here, Inc.* That's good news for me because there was no way I was getting through the firewall of this corporation, but at least now we know where the money's coming from. This connects two of our suspects—Rudman and Crivelli—to the same payer. What we need next is the articles of incorporation naming the officers."

"Wow, how fortunate. Nice work, Mel."

"Maybe it's fortunate, Joe, but I like to think of it as providence."

They were enjoying the moment until Mel's cell phone rang.

"Hello, Ms. Randle, I haven't heard from you for a while and I must confess my curiosity has been getting the better of me. I was wondering how your investigation was coming along."

"Professor Trudeau, what a surprise! I was *just* thinking of you as well."

"Ms. Randle, to be thought of by one of the most gifted students I have ever had the pleasure of teaching, I am honored. I have so many questions about your plans for the future and perhaps, while I'm in the DC area, we can get together. I may have an offer that would entice you."

Joe, who was listening at Mel's ear, had to prompt her to continue. She was wide eyed and frozen, knowing there had been no mention of Washington DC in the conversation.

"I'm honored you would take the time, Professor Trudeau."

"Oh, that's enough of the professor nonsense; besides, we may be colleagues soon—please call me Louie."

"Well, I'm honored, sir, and that may take a while, but please call me Mel; all my friends do. And I must say, Professor, now it's my curiosity that's aroused: when do you expect to arrive?"

"I'm actually flying in tomorrow at the request of an old friend who needs a bit of legal counsel. I guess he's been a naughty boy, but I suppose all that money and power can tempt even the best of people. You know, Mel, in Washington they don't even speak in terms of millions any longer, and I must admit when they start talking billions, it can make the best of us pay attention. Don't you agree, Mel?"

"Goodness, Professor Trudeau, now you really have my attention. Shall I meet you somewhere?"

"Actually, anticipating our good fortune, we are looking to lease an entire floor of a vacant office building and I'm dying to see it. Perhaps you could join us and we'll have a late dinner afterwards—my treat, of course."

"I look forward to seeing you again, sir. Please call me when you arrive and we'll confirm the time."

"By the way, Mel, as one prosecutor to another, do you think you have enough evidence to present a good case to the authorities?"

"Oh, I'm very close, Professor, very close. I'll fill you in when we have a chance to discuss things in person. Have a good flight, sir, and I'll see you soon."

As soon as she ended the call, they both collapsed into chairs.

"OH MY GOD! Did that really just happen?" screamed Mel.

By 6:00 PM, all the chickens came home to roost. Piper walked in with six hot meatball sub sandwiches, a huge Caesar salad, a twelve-pack of Amstel, and a large black man named Oscar.

"Hello, Oscar. Good to see you again."

"You too, Joe. I'm sure sorry about Gabby."

"I know, Oscar, we all are. Thanks for coming."

They passed out sandwiches and beer, ate salad out of paper bowls, and recapped the day.

The men were stuffing meatballs into their mouths, so Mel began.

"Nice work on Lonnie Rudman today, Colonel."

"You know I'm going to be a civilian soon and if you all don't mind, for the duration of this group, let's make it Nate instead of 'Colonel.' Is that all right?"

Everyone looked at him, shrugged their shoulders with their mouths full, and nodded in the affirmative. However, no one in the room could imagine for one second calling him Nate.

"All right then, we need to keep chipping away at that corporation and see if we can break through the layers of that sucker. I will say whoever designed it did a masterful job."

Joe wiped his face, took a slug of Amstel, and jumped in.

"I met with an old friend from the Agency today and she is really taking a risk but has agreed to see if she can find a common denominator between the names on our list, as well as the corporation. We should hear back by tomorrow. However, I may have something else.

"On my way back here, I suddenly remembered something and, for whatever reason, I missed it the first time. It was actually from you, Piper, when you came to Monterey to tell me about Gabby. You said she had just returned from Oregon where she had discovered something big. Apparently, whatever that was may have gotten her killed. Piper, I need you to think back and see if there was anything else anything to do with Oregon."

"Boy, I don't know, guys. Honestly, I was in shock and my mind just went numb. Right after her murder, I did hear some office scuttlebutt that she'd finally connected some dots, and it all had to do with Oregon. That clicked because a month earlier, I had flown her up there. The Agency had sprung for a Learjet because Gabby had insisted she was being followed and didn't want to fly commercial. Let me think about it for a second.

"She was... she was talking to me on the flight home and she said... she said, what a... what a con job. Yeah, that was it. She was talking about a politician, I think, who had pulled off some big scam and left office with a bunch of money. Yeah, that was it. She was absolutely giddy about it. I'm sorry, guys, I should have figured that out before tonight. Do you think it's important?"

Piper had been reminiscing with his eyes closed and his hands covering his face. When he lowered them, the others were all gathered behind Mel's laptop.

"All I did was type in 'Oregon, political con job' and I got fifty hits. And guess what, forty-nine of them are about a disgraced congressman who resigned and supposedly left town with ... wait a minute, can this be right...

'left town with his partner, and over one hundred million dollars.'"

"Holy guacamole, that's a lot of *dinero*."

"Yeah, I remember this," said Pike. "It was the whole Obama Care Exchange thing. It happened in several states, and if I recall, I think there was almost a billion dollars that went missing."

"Keep reading, Mel, what was this guy's name?"

"Here we go, *The Oregonian Newspaper*, let's see, three years ago...

"'After the collapse of the Affordable Health Care State Exchange, and an investigation into corruption, State Congressman Dr. John Grossman has resigned. While Dr. John denied any wrongdoing by himself or his longtime domestic partner...'

"Oh my God, BINGO!

"'...his longtime domestic partner, René Dumont. The scandal gained momentum when pictures surfaced of the two walking hand in hand in front of a million-dollar condo in Laguna Beach, California. The whereabouts of the couple is currently unknown.'

"Okay, hang on; let's type in 'Dr. John Grossman and René Dumont' and see if we can find something more current."

The results were story after story of the nonprofit ran by Dr. Grossman, his charitable work on behalf of suffering cancer patients, and the evolving treatments associated to cannabis. Also mentioned were his relentless efforts for a congressional mandate to legalize medical marijuana in all fifty states.

"Look, I'm new to the party," said Oscar, "but I'm guessing this is an aha moment, am I right?"

Mel stood, wrapped her arms around Joe's neck, and whispered, "We found him, Joe! We found René, and I'll bet you a bottle of good Oregon Tempranillo that he knows who killed Gabby."

Joe walked over to Piper who was still sitting on the couch.

"We were all numb, pal, but you came through for us, and it was a walk-off home run."

"All right, everyone, tomorrow's a big day so let's add Dr. John Grossman and René Dumont to the mix and tweak our plan."

At midnight, Joe received a text from Alex.

"Coffee—same place, 06:30."

Joe was waiting at the same table when Alex walked in. She smiled, said thanks for the coffee, and, as she turned to leave, she slid a small brown envelope across the table.

"Good seeing you again, Joseph; call me if you're ever off-duty."

He stuck the envelope in his pocket, waited until he finished his coffee, then walked to his car. He drove to a large parking lot, turned off the engine, and read the document from Alex. It was a copy of the articles of incorporation for an offshore IBC.

Name of Corporation:	North of Here, Inc.	
Type:	International Business Corporation	
Country of Origin:	Commonwealth of the Bahamas	
Registration Number:	(§80(8)-(10)).	
President:	René L. Dumont	51%
Secretary:	John T. Grossman	47%
Treasurer:	William C. Crivelli	2%

CHAPTER 37

The Army–Navy Game

"Hello, Mel. It's Louie; I hope I am not disturbing anything."

"Not at all, Professor Trudeau; I was expecting your call. I hope you had an enjoyable flight."

"Flying is not what it used to be, Mel, and I thought we agreed you were going to call me Louie."

"I'm really going to need some time to work on that, Professor Trudeau."

"Well, Mel, I have it on good authority you will probably have a great deal of time to work on it. I mentioned our conversation with my colleagues, and they are as excited as I am to discuss an offer I think you'll find too tempting to turn down. Enough of that for now: where can I pick you up this evening? We'll make a quick stop so you can see our new office building, and I know I'm being presumptuous, but maybe you could pick out a location for your office."

"Goodness, Professor... ah, Louie, you sure can be persuasive. However, I do have a few deadlines so if you will give me the address, I would be happy to meet you there. Then perhaps we can ride together to dinner—I mean if the offer is still good?"

Mel felt there was an uncomfortable pause, and thought she heard someone whispering.

"Certainly that would be fine; however, I must call you right back with the address, as I'm afraid you've caught me unprepared. Would that be all right?"

Once they had the address, Piper, Oscar, Pike, and Joe went over everything one more time.

The prospective office building was off Clara Baton Parkway, close to Glen Echo Park. It was suspiciously remote. The exterior, landscaping, and infrastructure of the office building had been tastefully completed, but inside, were large, unfinished rooms, left to the discretion of the tenants. However, the new office building was not the address given to Mel—that one was a half mile away.

They had agreed to meet at 6:00 PM and Mel's cab was running a few minutes late. The driver came to a stop and, as she was stepping out, the large imposing figure of Louis Trudeau blocked her exit.

"Good to see you again, Ms. Randle, but I must ask you to scoot across the seat."

To avoid being sat upon, Mel slid across as the professor entered the cab.

"I do apologize, Mel, but I'm afraid I muddled the address and now we are both late. But no worries, lass, it's only a short distance."

Before she could object, scream, or jump out, the professor gave the driver a new address, and they were on their way. It was all she could do to retain any facsimile of composure, but she did manage a smile.

"Mistakes do happen, don't they, Professor?"

"Yes, of course, my dear. The important thing is that they are not too costly. Ah, here we go—pull over right here, driver."

Mel noticed Louie as he glanced back to see if anyone was following. She also noticed how terribly dark the place was. The professor handed the driver a large bill and whispered something that Mel could not hear.

"Right this way if you please, Ms. Randle. I have the code for the door and we'll only be a jiffy. I've asked the cab to wait."

It didn't hurt, but the grip on her arm by the large man was uncomfortably firm. Once through the door, Mel was sure she heard the cab pull away.

Call it fate or dumb luck, but Lt. Col. Nathaniel Pike had gotten stuck behind an accident on MacArthur Boulevard and was ten minutes late. He parked two blocks east and, as he walked to his assigned position, he saw the cab with Mel and another man drive past. Pike was dressed in black and had crouched in the shadows when he saw the car pulling away from the curb. It only took a second to realize something was wrong. He turned again to see the taillights disappearing down the street. As he reached for his cell, a group text came through from Joe.

"She's late, has anyone seen anything?"

"She's gone!" he screamed. "She's in the taxi!" But no one heard.

Lt. Col. Pike had just turned forty and, for a man his age, was still militarily fit. However, as he sprinted the first two city blocks, watching the taillights turn at an intersection, his lungs were screaming for air. When he hurdled a fence, cutting through a parking lot, his legs began to ask permission to slow down. But there were the taillights of the cab again, and the shortcut had paid off. He finally had the good sense to speed-dial Joe's cell, but as he jumped off a curb, the phone slipped from his hand and slid down a grated storm drain.

"Nooooooo!"

Pike had to make a decision whether to stay and scream into a cavernous hole or continue to follow the cab. Looking up, he read the sign, yelled the street and Mel's name into the dark abyss, and took off like a man on fire.

As he rounded the next corner, he saw the cab leaving a building less than two blocks away. Once he was within one hundred yards, he pulled the pistol from his coat pocket and hugged the dark shadows close to the buildings. Looking toward the backside of the new office complex, he noticed faint light coming from somewhere inside the covered parking garage. Pike made his way around back, looking for a point of entry.

He stopped behind a dumpster, trying to control his breathing and get his emotions under control. As he considered their well-drafted plan, he could only shake his head and laugh. He approached the door, which was slightly ajar, and as he stuck his head inside, he was greeted by a familiar face.

"Hello, Pike. Whatever are you doing here?"

But before he could answer, a tire iron tore through his skull and, with thoughts of his beautiful wife, he slipped away.

"Ms. Randle, may I present a colleague of mine, Mr. René Dumont, and may I say, Mel, next to you, one of the brightest attorneys I've ever known."

"Ms. Randle, I've heard so much about you I feel as though we're old friends. I do hope you'll honor us and join our endeavors—our highly lucrative endeavors, I might add."

"Lucrative," interrupted Louie, "doesn't begin to paint a proper picture, Mel. They are throwing staggering amounts of money around Washington these days, and those wise enough to capitalize ... well, you get the idea."

All Mel could think about was stalling and not bursting into tears.

Joe, being a gifted sprinter, was only seconds behind Pike, and caught a glimpse of his friend as he had entered the rear of the parking garage.

"Gentlemen, I'm honored that you would consider me, but what I'd really like to hear is what exactly you do and what would be your expectations of me?"

"Ah, there is our contractor now."

"Good evening, everyone. Sorry I'm late and, to answer your question, Ms. Randle, I think you know exactly what we do, so let's stop the charades. It appears our guest of honor was expecting company, as you suspected, René, but I have delayed them."

As Joe was waiting on Oscar and Piper, he received an incoming text: "Just discovered another bit of info that might interest you. It appears

René has a brother, an ex-Navy SEAL whom I believe you've met—Retired Chief Petty Officer Mac Dumont. Please be careful, I think the guy's certifiably nuts. Alex."

Joe sent a group text informing the others that the targets were armed and extremely dangerous. He included the letters "SOS." It was not a distress call but the acronym for "Shoot on Sight." Then he carefully entered the back door leading to the stairwell—and found Pike lying in a large pool of blood. He took his pulse, found he was still alive, and dialed 911. After asking for an ambulance, he referenced Pike's rank and a possible Homeland Security issue. He wanted the entire cavalry coming.

Before the assault on Pike, there was only marginal evidence to indict the suspects. Now, however, there was attempted murder and, most likely, kidnapping.

"Goodness, Ms. Randle, what a shame. I suppose I knew all along; you're just a natural born prosecutor. Oh, well, let's wrap this up—I'm hungry."

René and Louie had Mel trapped in a corner of the room as she watched Mac pull a hypodermic syringe from his jacket pocket.

Joe heard his name whispered just as Piper glanced inside the doorway. He saw Pike lying on the floor and looked at Joe. Joe put a finger to his lips, nodded toward Pike, and mouthed the word "Help him." Piper nodded and Joe made his way up the steps until he heard talking. He eased through the door at the top of the stairs and had to catch it before it closed automatically. He let it ease shut and then, very cautiously, moved down the dark hallway toward the sound of an angry woman's voice.

"So, that's it then, you must be the asshole who killed Gabby."

"Please shut her up, Mac, it'll be one less loose end."

However, Mac, arrogant as he was, couldn't resist the temptation.

"Actually, I waved at her as I got out of my car. She even smiled, as if glad to see a friendly face, and then I shot her twice in the head."

"She was such a nosey-ninny," quipped René. "Why can't people just mind their own damned business?"

Mel was the only one who saw Joe slip into the room with his Glock at the ready position. He looked at her, nodded, then said, "Hello, Navy. It's been awhile."

Mac turned, with only a syringe in his hand, but still managed a cynical smile.

"Well, well... well, if the Rangers aren't here. Hello, Army. I sure hope you brought more than that little pistol or this isn't going to be much fun."

Both René and Louie had their backs to Joe, keeping an eye on Mel, and both were slowly reaching inside their waistbands for their weapons. What they counted on was Mac getting to Joe and killing him effortlessly. What they didn't count on was Mel being an undefeated, black-belt judo champion.

When she saw the pistol coming from Louie's pants, the sound began as a low guttural noise deep in her throat but rose as a deafening scream of ***"Kiai!"***

The sound reached the ears of Louie just as the side of Mel's foot dislodged his patella and completely severed the anterior cruciate ligament of his right knee. He screamed as he fell to the floor, and the distraction was just enough for Mac to slap the light switch, plunging the room into utter darkness.

Mel made another kick at René, but found only air. As Joe instinctively fell and rolled away from his position, he heard the six-inch blade swish above his head. Joe could not fire his weapon in the dark room for fear of hitting Mel. Everyone heard the sirens approaching from several directions. There was a very faint glow from beneath the door as someone had turned on the hallway light, but the room was still blacked out.

"Might as well give it up, Navy. There is no way you're getting out of this building. My team has all the exits covered and it sounds as if the cavalry's on its way. "

"Well, that's just the damned difference between Rangers and SEALs, Joe."

Joe could hear the voice moving ever so slowly but could not pinpoint his location due to the shrieks of Louie, who was still flopping around in excruciating pain. Nor did he know exactly where Mel or René was.

"You see, Joe, you Army boys are always looking for a chopper to retreat in, and us Navy Frogs don't figure we're doing our job until we're surrounded. Believe me, Army, I'm getting out and I'm taking this bitch of yours with me."

The sirens had become almost deafening as they surrounded the building. Somehow, Mac had found Mel in the darkness, put his knife to her throat, and eased her to her feet. It was not a good situation, but suddenly something very providential happened: René panicked. The dark room, the sirens, and Louie still screaming out in pain, were too much for his fragile nerves and he jerked the door open.

Suddenly light flooded in, and the very first rays lit up Mac's face as he stood behind Mel's right shoulder. He squinted and then screamed at his brother, but he never heard the sound of his own voice. Joe fired two shots from the Glock in such rapid succession it sounded like only one. Both 9-mm rounds entered Mac's right eye and slammed him into the blood-splattered wall. He slid to the ground just as another two rounds were fired outside the door.

"Clear!" yelled Joe.

"Clear!" came the response from Oscar as he held the door open and turned on a light.

Whether it was suicide or simply a foolhardy reaction, René had lifted his weapon in the direction of Agent Oscar Briggs, who put two close rounds into the man's heart.

Piper walked in as Mel was crying in Joe's arms. He looked at Oscar and said, "I sure could use a beer—how about you?"

Several city police officers and at least a half dozen FBI agents were combing the area as EMTs carried Louie down the stairs, handcuffed to a gurney. Senior FBI Agent Hawkins approached the four of them where they had huddled near the back of an ambulance.

"There's going to be a lot of questions and one hell of an investigation. I don't expect any of you will be leaving town anytime soon, right?"

They all agreed and asked if they could get a report on their friend, Lt. Col. Pike.

"They took him to George Washington University Hospital. If you all need a lift, I'm sure we can find you a ride."

"Our cars are just up the street, if you don't mind."

Oscar and Piper stopped and picked up Chinese, and Joe and Mel drove directly to the hospital. In less than thirty minutes, they were joined by Demi Pike who was trembling and white as a ghost. They held her hand and listened as she recounted her life with a career Air Force officer. An hour later, a trauma nurse walked through the double doors and approached them.

"You should all go home and get some sleep. The colonel will not be out of surgery for at least two more hours. However, I will tell you that he's in very critical condition and, if any of you believe in prayer, now would be a good time."

After she walked away, Mel stood and asked what they were waiting for. They all nodded, rose, and held hands.

It was sometime after 3:00 AM when the doctor laid a hand on Demi's foot. The five of them were sprawled out on two sofas, a chair, and the floor.

"I'm Dr. Abrahamson. Are you Ms. Pike?"

All five were standing, and all eyes were on the doc.

"You have a courageous fighter for a husband, Ms. Pike, but I have a feeling you knew that. The colonel is still in critical condition, but I expect it will be reduced to stable by 6:00 AM. We were able to remove all the bone fragments, repair his skull, and, as best as we can tell, he should make a full recovery. I might add, with as much blood as he lost, I think he is a very lucky man."

"Providence," said Piper. "We call it providence in this family."

CHAPTER 38

Loose Ends

At noon on the following day, Joe received a call from Special Agent Hawkins, whom he had met the previous night.

"I thought you might want to know—an ex-congressman from Oregon, by the name of Dr. John Grossman, was arrested an hour ago. Apparently he was trying to leave this thirty-eight-degree weather and board a flight to the Bahamas. Imagine that, vacationing in Nassau at a time like this, what a jerk."

At 5:00 PM the same day, District Attorney Archie Anderson notified Joe that FBI agents from the Portland office had detained businessman William Crivelli and Steelhead's city attorney, Kathy Sandburg, for questioning.

Moments later, he received a text from Diva asking if she could order more vanilla syrup and half-and-half.

A statement was released by the board of regents at Stanford Law School notifying students and facility that one of its own, Professor Luis Trudeau, PhD, had been arrested for crimes of a most heinous nature, and the entire board was both shocked and sickened by the news.

During a joint sting operation involving members of the DEA and Mexican Federales, arrests were made on several farms near Tijuana, Mexico. An announcement by Mexico's Deputy Secretary Munoz stated that longtime drug czar, Señor Javier Rivera, was killed in an exchange of gunfire with Mexican authorities.

Secretary Munoz was quoted saying, "While the US government played a minor role in the investigation, all arrests and convictions were strictly attributed to the hard work of his department."

It was decided by the attorney general the grieving families of Guatemala would be best served by the extradition of Tino Alverez. Unfortunately, the courts would not hear the case as he was stabbed to death in a Guatemala jail cell.

When Bennie Castro graduated from the Tijuana Institute of Technology with an associate's degree in computer science, he was wildly applauded by his family and good friend, Agent Paul Ruiz.

CHAPTER 39

Last Dance

Between the FBI, CIA, NSA, DEA, US Army, and an invitation to return and testify before a congressional subcommittee, the questions, interviews and paperwork had taken almost two weeks. Regardless of the demands, at the end of each day Joe, Mel, Oscar, and Piper met at the hospital to look in on Pike. As it turned out, according to the Pentagon, there had been a serious oversight with his paperwork, and his promotion to full bird colonel was unanimously approved. However, the inquiry cast light in several other dark corners. Congressmen and staffers from Colorado, California, and the state of Washington were brought before an ethics committee. One congressman, responsible for shutting down the original investigation, and who could not explain such a large infusion of cash to his reelection campaign, *"resigned due to personal matters."* Within a few months, two congressmen were censured by their peers, four staffers were fired, and more than one head rolled at the Pentagon. All in all, for Washington DC, it was some unusual, but necessary housekeeping.

During a tearful goodbye dinner in Colonel Pike's hospital room, the five *amigos* shared pizza and, to Piper's chagrin, a six-pack of Dr. Pepper.

"I was reading this morning," said the colonel, "from a book I received from Joe, that, in order to see the extraordinary view from the sun-washed mountaintops, we have to walk through the dark valleys. It also said we don't walk alone. I want each of you to know that God and I will always be there, to walk through the valleys with you."

All too often, exceptional moments are denigrated by words. They all nodded their heads, knowing there was nothing more to be said.

The homecoming at Segundo Vida Vineyards was perfect—a low-key affair with family and only the best of friends. Lizzie, Jillian, and Sonata made carne asada, homemade tamales, and chili verde with all the trimmings. The outside fireplace roared, the wine flowed, the laughter was contagious, and Jose and Sonata sang.

As the warmth of the fire took the chill out of the February evening, Joe leaned close to Mel and Mel leaned back.

"What do you think—District Attorney Michele Randle does have a nice ring to it."

"Yeah, Joe, about that. I was thinking maybe I should head back down to California for a while. You know, spend some time with my family and take a break. It's been a pretty exciting few months, and I thought maybe a change of scenery would be good for me."

The words poured over Joe's heart like a dark, rain cloud intruding on an outdoor wedding. The laughter and singing continued but he could no longer hear it.

The idea of Mel leaving had never occurred to him, but, suddenly, he had to face the realization. After all Mel was a visitor, and unexpected circumstances had snatched her, holding her captive from her own dreams. That's it, a reluctant prisoner, finally free of a nightmarish fantasy. Of course, she wants to run, anyone would. The certainty exploded through Joe's mind in a matter of seconds. Instantly, it was painfully clear: while he couldn't bear the idea of her leaving, he had no right to ask her to stay.

"Joe ... *Joe* ... hello! Anyone home?"

The sound of his father's voice appeared distant but suddenly snapped him back to reality.

"Goodness, son, where were you? You looked to be a million miles away. As I was saying, it's one of your favorites—why don't you ask Mel to dance?"

Joe held her close and felt the tears as they rolled onto his cheek.

"It won't be the same, you know. The conversations will pale, the coffee won't taste as good, and I'll always be looking toward the door."

The following morning, Joe found a note, slipped under the door of his coffee shop.

"I explained to Archie and Hobie that I needed some time.

They were sweet and told me they understood. I'll call your parents from the road and tell them goodbye.

I'm sorry, Joe; I couldn't risk seeing you again.

I will cry all the way to California, but I need to do this.

Thank you for helping me believe again,

you are my providence ___________

And, Joseph Chandler, you take my breath away."

Forever, Mel

Epilogue

When he looked up and saw the tears in Diva's eyes, the moment would be forever seared in his mind.

"Joe Chandler, if you don't go get that sweet girly girl, I just know you'll regret it."

He already did, and as badly as he wanted to call her, chase her, and beg her to stay, something more powerful, a voice untethered by emotion, spoke deep to the storm raging in his soul—*"Peace, be still."*

The End

Author's Note

Gringo Joe is a work of fiction. The names, characters, places, and incidents portrayed in the story are random and often spontaneous products of the author's vivid imagination. Any resemblance to actual persons, living or deceased, businesses, companies, corporations, locations, or events is entirely coincidental. While the settings may reflect some of the places I have lived or traveled, I have no grievances, grudges, or axes to grind with anyone or any locale. It has been my pleasure to travel extensively, and as is my nature, I've looked for the best in each place, and always found it. As is the case with many fictional writers, my works blend the factual with the unimaginable in hopes of weaving an enjoyable story.

Remember, if there are lies, there is truth, if there is darkness, there is light, and if there is evil, there is goodness. There is no lie so big, no place so dark, or evil so great, that God cannot ransom you—absolutely none

JD Davis

Credits

1. *CBS News.* "What's the preferred weed? Mexican or American?" CBS, March 17, 2015
2. Rugg, Peter. "Legal American Weed Is Undercutting Mexican Drug Cartel Profits: Yet another reason to hope for more legalization in the 2016." December 30, 2015. *Inverse. https://www.inverse.com/article/9740-legal-american-weed-is-undercutting-mexican-drug-cartel-prof.*
3. Burnett, John. "Legal Pot In The U.S. May Be Undercutting Mexican Marijuana." December 1, 2014. *All Things Considered: NPR. https://www.npr.org/sections/parallels/2014/12/01/367802425/legal-pot-in-the-u-s-may-be-undercutting-mexican-marijuana.*
4. Hudak, John, PhD and Grace Wallace. "Ending the U.S. government's war on medical marijuana research." Effective Public Management at Brookings. October 20, 2015. *Brookings. https://www.brookings.edu/wp-content/uploads/2016/06/Ending-the-US-governments-war-on-medical-marijuana-research.pdf.*
5. Little Richard. *Lucille.* Cowritten by Albert Collins. Released 1957. Los Angeles: Specialty Records.
6. *The Blues Brothers.* Directed by John Landis. Universal Pictures, 1980.
7. Craig, Tim. "U.S. troops dispatched to Kunduz to help

Afghan forces". September 30, 2015. *Washington Post. https://www.washingtonpost.com/world/asia_pacific/us-troops-dispatched-to-kunduz-to-help-afghan-forces/2015/09/30/ea7768f2-66e5-11e5-9223-70cb36460919_story.html?utm_term=.aab0adf01a01.*

8. Smurf. "Mexican Cartels Buying Afghan Heroin." January 5, 2011. *Borderland Beat. http://www.borderlandbeat.com/2011/01/mexican-cartels-buying-afghan-heroin.html.*
9. *The Holy Bible, English Standard Version.* Wheaton: Crossway, 2016
10. *The Holy Bible, New Living Translation.* Carol Stream: Tyndale House Publishers, Inc., 2015
11. Beck, Brandon and Mark Merrill. *League of Legends.* Los Angeles: Riot Games, Inc., 2015. *https://na.leagueoflegends.com/en/.*
12. Petty, Tom. *Free Fallin'.* Cowritten by Jeff Lynne. Released 1989. Universal City: MCA Records.
13. Third Day. *I Need a Miracle.* Written by Mac Powell, Mark Lee, David Carr, and Tai Anderson / Produced by Brendan O'Brien. Released 2012. Brentwood: Capitol Christian Music Group.
14. Winslow, Don. *The Power of the Dog.* New York: Alfred A. Knopf, Inc., 2005
15. Winslow, Don. *The Cartel.* New York: Alfred A. Knopf, Inc., 2015

CPSIA information can be obtained
at www.ICGtesting.com
Printed in the USA
LVHW02*1910050718
582702LV00002B/3/P